"What exactly are you doing?" she asked without preamble.

"I'm...taking a break?" Leo said, indicating the room with a wave of his hand.

"Funny. I mean, what are you doing here? In my hospital? In my clinic?" She pointed at the ground before her in emphasis. "I don't hear hide or hair from you in years and all of a sudden, you're everywhere I turn?"

"I told you I'd been hired by the hospital. I didn't exactly catch you by surprise."

"After you showed up in my clinic out of the blue. Leo, it's been years. Do you understand that?" Her eyes narrowed at him. "You got married."

That was an oddly specific detail for her to cling to at this moment, but he played along, if only to know where her brain was headed. "I *was* married."

Nati blinked twice. "You're not...married anymore?"

"Divorced, I believe they called it." He shook out his head, trying to catch the thread of her earlier accusation. "What do you care? You broke up with me. Why would I be following you anywhere? You made it clear that you didn't want anything to do with me."

Dear Reader,

The series that began with Valeria Navarro in
A Delicious Dilemma and continued with Rafael in
The Best Man's Problem finally comes full circle
with Natalía in *The Trouble with Exes*. In the third
book of the Navarro family series, Nati, the youngest
Navarro, has to reckon with her past when her ex, Leo
Espinoza, reappears in her life.

Nati has worked hard to reach her goal of becoming a
practicing ER physician in East Ward General Hospital
despite being the first doctor in the family and
overcoming a learning disability.

She is no stranger to the sacrifices required to
become a doctor. That's why she could never have
let Leo give up the chance to accept a prestigious
residency on the other side of the country years
earlier, especially when he was willing to give it all up
for her. She did what she had to do and ended their
relationship before Leo made a decision he would
regret.

Now Leo's back, and so are all the feelings Nati
thought she'd buried.

A common thread that runs through each novel is the
Navarros' willingness to make sacrifices for the ones
they love, and Nati is no different. But sacrifices have
nothing to do with feelings, which have a bad habit of
showing up when you least expect them.

Get ready to return to East Ward and the Navarro
family as they navigate the complexities of family,
culture and community to find love that lasts.

Thank you for choosing *The Trouble with Exes*!

Sera Taíno

The Trouble with Exes

SERA TAÍNO

HARLEQUIN

SPECIAL
EDITION

HARLEQUIN®

SPECIAL EDITION™

Recycling programs
for this product may
not exist in your area.

ISBN-13: 978-1-335-72464-9

The Trouble with Exes

Copyright © 2023 by Sera Taíno

For questions and comments about the quality of this book, please contact us at CustomerService@Harlequin.com.

Harlequin Enterprises ULC
22 Adelaide St. West, 41st Floor
Toronto, Ontario M5H 4E3, Canada
www.Harlequin.com

Printed in U.S.A.

Sera Taíno writes Latinx romances exploring love in the context of family and community. She is the 2019–2020 recipient of the Harlequin Romance Includes You Mentorship, resulting in the publication of her debut contemporary romance, *A Delicious Dilemma*. When she's not writing, she can be found teaching her high school literature class, crafting, and wrangling her husband and two children.

Books by Sera Taíno

Harlequin Special Edition

The Navarros

A Delicious Dilemma
The Best Man's Problem

Visit the Author Profile page
at Harlequin.com for more titles.

To my Italian vacation.
You're the only reason I got this book done on time.

And to Stephanie Doig, for getting me the time I needed.
Thank you for your support.

Chapter One

Nati

The call came through around midnight. Nati stared longingly at the steaming-hot liquid of her fresh coffee, swearing under her breath because she knew that when she came back for it, the coffee would have gone cold. She'd have to either heat it up or dump it out and make a new cup, running the risk that she'd be thwarted yet again in her quest to consume as much caffeine as the human body could sustain.

"I'm not finishing this cup, am I?" Nati murmured, setting it down on the counter of the break room.

"Forecast isn't looking favorable at the moment, Dr. Navarro," said Dr. Caleb Carter. He was more than just her fellow physician on duty. He was also Nati's friend and former med school classmate. He scooped up her mug together with his and dumped out the coffee, rinsing and setting both cups to dry.

"Ready?" he asked.

"Duty calls." Nati followed him out of the break room and to the examination area. They took turns washing their hands before donning surgical gloves and strapping their masks tightly in place.

"How about setting up an IV drip directly into your veins?" Caleb said.

Nati snorted. "Director says it violates some health code or other. Trust me, I asked."

"No coffee IVs, then," Caleb's long brown fingers adjusted Nati's mask before he put on his own. "We'll just have to consume the burnt variety the good old-fashioned way."

Caleb would know about good coffee. He'd been born in Atlanta, his father Southern black and his mother Dominican. Like Nati's Puerto Rican family, they knew good coffee—and rum—when they tasted it.

"Let's go earn our salary." Nati put on her game face as she picked up the chart from the nurses' station and made her way to the patient area.

"Tahira is probably in bed," Nati complained when she looked at the time. Dr. Tahira Hadid was the trauma surgeon on call. She was part of Nati's tightly knit friendship group forged in the fires of medical school. They'd studied together and competed against each other for the best grades until they graduated, when they went their separate ways to complete their respective specializations and residencies.

There had been a fourth member of their crew once. But Caleb and Tahira never talked about Leo Espinoza. Her ex-boyfriend and once love of her life was now best left in the past, the one member of their group who had gotten away.

The one member of their group Nati had pushed away.

Even after six years, Nati still couldn't go one day without thinking of Leo.

Nati scanned the chart in front of her. Adult man. Respiratory distress. Chronic illnesses include high blood pressure and pancreatic cancer. Possible cardiac distress—

Her beeper went off. She had only to flash a glance at the code on her device to switch modes.

"Code Blue," Caleb confirmed just as nurses converged on the patient in room 5. A familiar instinct took over Nati, one that always kicked in when an emergency landed in her ER. Nonmedical people tended to panic, their hearts racing and breathing elevated—all signs of a loss of control. Not Nati. When the pressure was highest, Nati became the coldest, most fundamental version of herself. Levelheaded. Calculated. Unerring. The adrenaline had the effect of focusing her senses so that all she saw was the patient in front of her—not as a person, but as a collection of conundrums to be unraveled and addressed as quickly and precisely as possible.

Caleb was already administering CPR while her

head nurse was running an IV and another prepared the AED. Nati barked out orders as she examined the patient—older Latino, aged seventy. Signs of muscular atrophy and weight loss. Blood pressure dropping like a stone. Erratic breathing and edema in his extremities. Nati focused on the immediate as she began chest compressions.

It took Nati's team fifteen minutes to fully stabilize patient, who gained consciousness twice before sinking into the typical fatigue of someone experiencing a cardiac event. Nati wiped her brow with the sleeve of her coat.

"Can we get him upstairs?" she asked the nurse on duty. Nati had once gone feral with admin when several of her patients had to be boarded after hospital beds had been reduced in the name of cost cutting. Her patients had ended up spending the night in gurneys parked along the hallways. The poor nurse must have heard about Nati because she looked like she expected to get her head bitten off.

"They're accelerating a discharge, Dr. Navarro. Room 5 should be admitted soon."

"Good," Nati said, making notes in the chart, finally taking a moment to absorb the details of the person she'd just treated. A cold dread crept across her chest. "No way," she muttered to herself. Then louder to no one in particular, "Where's Dr. Carter?"

"Dr. Carter is right here," came Caleb's familiar deep voice.

"Is the family of room 5 outside?" She handed the chart to him.

He scanned the chart quickly, understanding cascading over his features. "Raul Alonzo Espinoza. Isn't that…?"

Nati glanced back into the patient's room. She hadn't recognized Leo's father—not with the ravages of age, illness and distress masking his once youthful features. And when Nati went into treatment mode, she filtered out every detail except the ones she needed to stabilize the patient. Her focus was on getting them out of her emergency room so their journey to long-term healing could begin.

"It's Dr. Espinoza, Leo's father," she said, holding back the quiver in her voice. Raul had always been kind to her the few times they'd met when she was still dating Leo.

Caleb took a slow, deep breath. "Well, damn. How long, Nati?"

Nati was still processing the presence of Dr. Raul Espinoza in her ER, but she understood the implicit question. *How long has it been since you've seen Leo?*

"Six years."

That last time, they were walking away from each other after a sudden and total breakup. In the moment, it had seemed like the right decision—ending things with Leo so they could each be free to pursue opportunities that only came once in a lifetime: for him, a prestigious residency in UCLA; for her, NYU Langone's Ronald O. Perelman Department of Emergency Medicine, a program close to her family and the community that meant so much to her. It hadn't been an easy decision, and Leo had fought her on it, but she was not going to be the one to hold either of them back, no matter how much it hurt them both.

Nati had done what she thought was the right thing and broken things off, pretending that it hadn't sundered her into two pieces. A heartbreak Leo clearly hadn't felt, because he'd gotten married within six months of breaking up and had stayed in California ever since.

"At the very least, Genevieve will be with him." Last Nati had heard, Genevieve, Leo's sister, was still living in East Ward to be close to their parents. Leo's parents had divorced when they were young and had remained on good terms, co-parenting Leo and Genevieve. Nati imagined she'd also be seeing Leo's mother, Dr. Zoraida Espinoza. Zoraida had never been a big fan of Nati's when she and Leo had dated, and Zoraida had been vocal about her opinions.

Nati scrubbed her face, belatedly remembering that she had actually put some makeup on to cover her sun-deprived skin, which was normally a golden brown when she wasn't working herself to the bone. She rubbed the black specks of mascara from her fingertips. "I have to go out there and talk to them. Want to come?"

Caleb sighed. "ER has slowed down a little. I can cover for you if you need time."

Nati looked up at her friend. "What if Leo's here?" The chances were low, but it was a possibility to consider.

"Doubt it. He hasn't been back since he left," Caleb said quietly. "He forgot about us."

Nati's heart ached with guilt. Out of the three of them, Caleb had been the one who'd known Leo the longest; they'd gone to the same high school together before Caleb had transitioned. Nati was heartbroken when Leo left, but it had been her wish. Caleb had had nothing to do with that, and yet, Leo had left without saying goodbye to his friends or reaching out to them in the six years that had passed.

Nati put a hand on Caleb's shoulder. He patted it, as if she was the one in need of comforting. Though Caleb was too kind to say so, this was Nati's fault as well.

After her conversation with Caleb, Nati made her way directly to the worn emergency room waiting area. East Ward General Hospital was the first hospital built in East Ward, parts of it added or renovated as needed over the decades. The emergency department was part of the original construction and, despite modernizations, showed signs of its age in its uneven walls and white-worn-to-gray tile.

From across the waiting area, Nati recognized Genevieve and Zoraida, huddled together on two plastic orange chairs. While Zoraida hadn't been too impressed with Nati, Genevieve had always been kind to her. When things ended with Leo, Nati had lost her as well.

"Nati?" Genevieve said, coming slowly to her feet. "What are you…?" Genevieve's eyes swept Nati up and down, taking in her white jacket and the badge with her name, Dr. Natalia Navarro, etched into the faux metal. "Well, look at you." Genevieve had been working on a master's degree in creative writing when Nati and Leo were med students, but even with their different career interests they'd always gotten along.

Zoraida, on the other hand, barely looked at Nati.

Nati called on all her composure before speaking. "Genevieve. Zoraida. It's good to see you both again. I just wish it were under different circumstances."

Genevieve stepped forward, giving Nati a hug that smelled like Lysol and peaches. Her wavy auburn hair was tied back in a messy bun, ringlets of rust-red curling over her neck. "It's been too long," she said when she pulled back.

Nati choked back a sob, burying it as she did all her unpleasant feelings. She had missed their friendship and tried not to let the grief of so many lost moments keep her from doing her job.

"How is Raul?" Zoraida interjected without preamble. She was an elegant woman in slacks and a button-up shirt, a sharp contrast to Genevieve's unruly hair, jeans and T-shirt combination. Zoraida had composure down to an art. Only the twisting together of her hands gave away her worry for her ex-husband's well-being.

"Dr. Espinoza had a cardiac event. We were able to stabilize him, but we will be admitting him to the hospital for evaluation."

"He has stage 2 pancreatic cancer," Genevieve said. "Would that have anything to do with tonight?"

Nati's heart plummeted at the confirmation of what she'd seen on Raul's chart. "I'm sorry about that diagnosis."

"It's highly likely," Zoraida interrupted, crossing

her arms. "But we won't know until further tests are done, will we?"

Nati nodded. "Correct. He will remain until those results come back."

Zoraida nodded before turning away from Nati to look out the window of the waiting room, hugging herself against the chill…or the fear.

Genevieve mouthed, "I'm sorry," To which Nati only shrugged. She didn't want to be bitter, but it was hard to forget how Zoraida had dismissed Nati as Leo's love interest all those years ago. Nati's family didn't meet Zoraida's standards—her father's working-class background, their deceased mother, Nati's efforts to win scholarships and grants wherever she could in spite of her dyslexia…all were factors that were not in her favor. The fact that Nati's degree was the consequence not only of her own determination to finish and excel but also a testament to her family's unyielding support meant nothing to Zoraida.

Nati had to force down that old resentment and situate herself in the present. She would address Leo's mother with the professionalism she'd cultivated over years of study. She tried to remember that, despite their strained history, Zoraida was dealing with a terminally ill ex-husband who'd had a cardiac event. Nati needed to find the patience to deal with her.

"Mami, I got here as soon as I heard," came a deep voice from the swishing doors of the emergency room. Nati turned and watched as six years of her life evaporated before her eyes.

"Leo," she breathed.

Leo came to a halt before Nati. She found herself face-to-face with familiar green eyes framed under long, dark lashes that, even after all these years, sparkled with familiarity. With a medium build, he had a few inches on Nati without heels. He held his expression tight, the lines of his olive skin marred with worry. His russet-colored hair that turned to a ruddy copper red in the summer was a tousled mess, his black sweatpants and white T-shirt appearing more like pajamas than streetwear.

Six years, Nati thought. Six years since she'd sent him away. Had she conjured him from the desperate depths of their past? Fallen into a daydream constructed of a patchwork of her current situation knitted to old desires and distant memories? She forced herself to concentrate on her purpose for being there.

"Nati?" Leo asked.

"Leo. It's been a long time," Nati said.

Leo didn't stop staring at her until his mother cleared her throat. Leo jerked to awareness and asked, "You're here?"

"I'm the physician on staff tonight," she said, grasping her clipboard to her chest to steady herself. "I… we stabilized your father."

"Dr. Roberts will be here soon," Zoraida said from her vantage point near the window. "He'll know how to better handle your father's medical condition."

Better than me. Zoraida was right. Dr. Roberts was part of Raul's treatment team, according to the information provided by his family. He would be better able to treat him long term.

However, Nati understood the subtext in Zoraida's eyes. Anyone was better than Nati.

Leo seemed to want to say more. Maybe ask questions like the ones that were racing through her mind—why was he here and not in California, the place he'd called home for the last six years? What had his life been like all this time? Did he think of her sometimes, the way she did him?

But he didn't ask. There were more important things to worry about.

"Is Papá okay?" he asked, his gaze lingering as if Nati's face had the answers to all his questions, before turning to his mother and sister.

"He's stable," Zoraida answered.

"Because of Nati. She was on the code team," Genevieve said, giving Leo a recap of Nati's assessment. Nati remained quiet, keeping her professional armor intact, the one she put on when she had to be Dr. Navarro—cool and competent, even if inside, she was shaking with uncertainty. Zoraida asked pointed questions, as Nati would expect her to do, given her own professional expertise and her relationship with Raul, which was still amicable despite the divorce.

"I'll go home and pick up some of his things," Genevieve said.

Nati watched as Genevieve gave her mother and brother a quick hug before heading out through the swishing glass doors. Nati wanted to tell her to wait, that it was too late to be running around East Ward, but her beeper vibrated. Reading the message, she knew she couldn't linger any longer.

Nati made to leave, allowing Leo and his mother to have a moment of privacy, but Leo's voice pulled her back again.

"How long until we can see him?" Leo asked. Her heart ached for him, but she wasn't allowed to comfort him anymore. She was no longer allowed to be anything other than his father's attending physician, and even that for only a few hours more.

Nati cleared her suddenly dry throat. "I'll have someone bring you back to see him shortly."

Leo excused himself with his mother and walked alongside Nati, keeping her from bolting in the direction of the emergency department.

"Nati, I'm… Wow, this is a lot. I had no idea you were the ER physician on call. Congratulations, by the way. I know you wanted to work in a hospital that would allow you to be close to your family."

Nati's thoughts moved sluggishly through a fog of disbelief. She couldn't afford to become disoriented by Leo's presence. She was in a hurry and would soon have to get into work mode, which left no room for all the questions that were jockeying for space in her brain. "Thanks. I heard you're still at UCLA. That must be amazing."

"It is," Leo said. "I run an experimental surgical lab, one of the few of its kind in the world."

That made Nati both wildly happy and excruciatingly sad at the same time. It's what she'd wanted for him—to be able to excel and rise to the top of his field. Her sadness was for her alone, that she'd had to live without him.

"I really have to get going," Nati said, walking with more resolution.

"Right. Of course, you're on the job. I just… I appreciate you being there for Papá. I know he was in the best possible hands."

"Thank you," Nati said, unable to find any other words to answer him. She was still convinced that the last hour hadn't happened, that this was all a caffeine-fueled daydream she had yet to shake herself out of. Leo, here, in East Ward? Nati nearly dropped the security badge that opened the sealed reception doors allowing her back inside the emergency department. She welcomed the frenetic work that awaited her, if nothing more than to drown out her conflicting feelings about the reappearance of an ex she thought she'd never see again.

Chapter Two

Leo

"That was an unpleasant surprise," Mamá said, managing to look elegant despite having been called out of bed to accompany a terrified Genevieve to the hospital with her father.

"Ma, please." Leo didn't think he could handle his mother at the moment. He sank into the hard plastic chair of the waiting area, debating whether or not to flex his medical credentials to gain access to his father's room sooner, if only to allow his mother to check his chart and give them all something else to think about besides Nati.

"I'm not saying anything you don't know. You dodged a bullet, *mijo*, that's all." Mamá took the seat next to him, settling in for a conversation he wasn't in the mood to have. "I knew there was a risk of seeing her, but I was so worried about your father." She sucked her teeth, turning her face to the window, even though there was nothing to see there but her reflection and the darkness beyond.

So Mami knew Nati was working at EWGH. It didn't surprise him—his mother was well connected after a lifetime of medical practice in East Ward, and it was the sort of thing she would know. What she could not have imagined was that Leo had been quietly following Nati's career for years. He hadn't processed what seeing Nati again would mean, but he had been vaguely aware of the possibility. However, he certainly was not going to have that conversation with his mother, of all people, given how dead set she'd been against Nati from the very beginning.

"Nati is in the past. No one is thinking like that anymore," Leo said.

"Are you sure? Because a girl like that would love nothing more than to—"

Leo stood suddenly. He didn't have it in him to relive his mother's digs at Nati, to listen to her assassinate Nati's character. It was as unbearable now as it had been then. "I'm going to see how long we have to wait before seeing Papá." He didn't listen for her response, but made his way across the tiled waiting area. If he could speak to the receptionist, he might persuade her to let at least his mother in to see his father. However, despite a heavy dose of charm, she gave him the same answer Nati had given him.

Instead of returning to where his mother sat, he stepped outside into the warm air. It was nearing two in the morning, the normally bustling streets now covered in sparse traffic. He regretted letting Genevieve leave at this hour, blaming the stress over his father, sleeplessness and Nati's appearance for the brain fog he was experiencing. Leo's exhaustion was getting the best of him. His patience for everything, including his mother, had simply vanished.

This time last month, Leo had been in California, still recovering from his divorce the year before and working as a surgical fellow at UCLA's Medical Center, a prestigious position that ensured he would consistently work more hours than was healthy. It was his dream job, and over the years, he'd managed to cobble together a collection of friends that formed the foundation of his rather meager social life.

Then, Papá's illness had come at him like an out-of-control semi smashing into Leo's life. He'd arranged an immediate leave of absence, taken his sister up on her offer to let him stay with her and come back to his hometown of East Ward after six years. He had never felt like more of a stranger. When he'd left, his father had been an active, healthy man in his sixties. Now, his sister and mother were caring for someone who looked years older with barely half the strength of before.

Leo's entire focus had been on his family, so he was not prepared to see Nati Navarro again. Even though he could say almost down to the hour when she started working at EWGH, and had kept track of her life through the years, he'd never had any intention of actively looking for her. She'd made it clear when she'd broken up with him six years earlier that she didn't love him anymore. Even when he'd begged her to reconsider, she'd been adamant, making him understand that their relationship had not been worth fighting for. Why would he go after her when she had so easily excised him from her life?

At least his mother had been thrilled over the breakup. She had never accepted Nati for Leo and had been obvious about it. His mother had found Nati too brash, too outspoken and without the kind of family his mother would want to display to the world. When Nati and Leo's relationship came to an end, it was all Leo could do to keep her from throwing a party to celebrate. She'd been the one who brought Michelle onto his radar at just the right moment, leading to their sudden and ill-conceived marriage.

But now he was back, where his past had decided to make a reappearance.

His sister racing up the walk caught him unawares. Her mane of hair was pulled into a neat high ponytail, but otherwise, she was just as sloppily dressed as he was, wearing jeans and a long-sleeved pink shirt featuring a rabbit holding a coffee cup. She pulled a small carry-on luggage bag behind her, no doubt full of anything his father might need.

"Let me get that," he said, taking the bag from her.

"What are you doing out here? Have there been any changes?"

Leo shook his head. "No changes. I'm just getting some fresh air."

Genevieve twisted her hands together. "And to get a break from Mom. I'll bet she had a lot to say after she saw Nati."

"If you had bet, you would have won." His mother's words came back to him, and despite all the pain Nati's breakup had caused him, he knew she did not deserve his mother's harsh judgment. There was something good and true in Nati. Even if she hadn't wanted to be with him anymore, it didn't change the core of who she was. This innate goodness is what had made it so hard to forget about Nati. She had always been the best person he'd ever known.

"After all these years, I don't understand why Mamá hates Nati so much."

Genevieve gave a mirthless laugh. "It's not Nati she hates. It's the concept of Nati."

"Not everyone can trace their family history back to the foundation of the island," Leo nearly growled in irritation. Their mother came from a well-to-do family, but the Revolution had forced them to flee. That disdain and mistrust for anyone deemed of a lower class was a leftover from the stories her mother had heard in her childhood, stories that she'd never outgrown. She simply could not see the value in Nati's persistence and hard work, how it had paid off when she had earned not only a medical degree with top grades, but also a residency at an NYU hospital. All Mamá saw was an upstart with no family pedigree to speak of, trying to achieve social mobility by marrying into the Espinoza family.

"Well, Mom can calm down. She's in no danger from Nati," Leo said. Genevieve stared at him for several seconds before looking away, lapsing into silence. His sister saw right through him, but to his relief, she let the matter rest for now. There was so much noise and upheaval in their lives already that these quiet moments between them were precious.

After a time, Genevieve asked, "Do you think he's going to be okay?" Her voice had gone tinny, almost plaintive. Leo's heart twisted in his chest. Genevieve was always going to be the little sister he had promised to keep safe, but their father's illness was something he could not protect her from.

"We can only hope he will be," Leo answered.

Genevieve hugged herself. "I'm so worried."

Leo pulled his sister against him, tucking her messy bun under his chin. "Everything will work out like it's supposed to."

Genevieve snuffled against his shirt. "Like it's supposed to, but not how we want it to."

"Leo," came his mother's voice. "They've admitted your father. We should go."

Leo left a kiss on the top of his sister's head before releasing her and turning to find Mamá waiting, looking suddenly very small. He instantly regretted his earlier anger. His mother could be difficult and judgmental, hardened by the struggles of a Latina trying to hold her own in a world full of white male surgeons quick and ready to put her in her place. But she was indescribably sweet at times, and so vulnerable, he couldn't help but want to take care of her as well. He put an arm around Mamá's shoulder, waving his sister over to tuck her into his other side, and prepared to see his father.

* * *

Papá lay peacefully in his hospital bed, machinery punctuating the antiseptic room with whirrs and beeps to which he was completely oblivious. He did not stir at his family's arrival, nor for the nurse who stood at the foot of the bed writing notes in his chart.

Leo had been back in East Ward for only two weeks and had barely gotten used to his father's deterioration. Seeing him like this was twice as difficult, and he had to bite back the tears that welled up. This was not Dr. Raul Espinoza, the same man who, in his twenties, had the courage to escape a hotel room in Miami on a diplomatic visit, defecting from Castro's medical army with nothing more than his licence to practice medicine, a few dollars in his pocket and the clothes on his back. The same man who had set himself a goal of perfecting his English in one year, and who had taken the endless exams that would validate his medical training and allow him to become a doctor in the US.

The man in the bed was a diminished version of his father, and it made Leo sad that he had spent these last few years so far from him.

Papá had always loved Nati. Contrary to his mother, Papá appreciated Nati's drive and had real admiration for her accomplishments. His father had said that she was the type of woman with her feet on the ground and her head held high. When Nati broke up with Leo, it took Papá a long time to accept it, even after he'd already married Michelle.

The rustling of Mamá picking up Raul's chart after the nurse left pulled him from his thoughts. She examined the notes and treatment written there before setting it down. "Everything seems to be in order," she sniffed.

"I try to be as thorough as possible," came Nati's voice through the open door.

Mamá looked up and gave her a curt nod before taking up a place near Papá's side. Genevieve gave Nati a small smile and asked her to step outside into the hallway, the two women speaking in quiet tones. This left Leo to flail alone in the center of the room.

God, Nati had changed. The sweet, girlish look from years past had given way to that of a person who had grown into her authority. This change was evident in her stance, the confident way she spoke, the sparkle of intelligence in her eyes. She had always outstripped him and everyone else academically throughout their medical school years. She was dyslexic, but no one who hadn't seen her ruthlessly employ the strategies she'd constructed over a lifetime to keep on top of her studies would have known by watching her now; she was all composure and expertise.

It didn't help that she was also more incandescently beautiful than ever. Her golden curls, pulled back in a ponytail, looked like melted bronze as she moved, shimmering under the dull cast of phosphorescent lighting, her eyes the color of honey rimmed with dark brown. And her skin—Leo couldn't shake the memory of the way her soft, fawn-colored skin had once felt under his palms, the silken firmness of it, the supple way it absorbed both his gentlest and roughest touch.

Leo shook himself out of the past and approached

his father's bed. He had no right to think about Nati that way, and this was neither the time nor the place. Even if Nati seemed to sneak glances at him whenever he looked away, he counted that as curiosity, much like him trying to understand what had changed about her. A desire to see if the reality of who she was now matched with the idea he'd had of her all those years ago.

It didn't matter. She'd broken up with him, made it clear that she didn't think their relationship was worth saving and left him so emotionally wrecked that he hadn't been able to think straight for months. She had no effect on him anymore.

And yet, just the memory of those dark days after Nati made his heart race, his entire body echoing with the pain of it in a way it might not have if he wasn't already flayed alive by his father's hospitalization.

Genevieve caught his attention and waved him to the door, but he pretended not to see—he suddenly didn't want to speak to Nati for fear that if he did, he might say something inappropriate or demand answers to questions he hadn't asked in a long time, answers he didn't know he still needed. Questions like, why hadn't she fought harder for their relationship? What had he done so wrong to make her stop loving him from one day to the next?

His mother was holding a quiet vigil on the other side of his father's bed. Leo touched his father's hand, feeling the clammy cold of his fingers. He pulled the blanket up, tucking him in. He was aware of Nati's presence behind him when she reentered the room with his sister, but he ignored it, trying not to respond to the inevitable pull. Leo sharpened his focus—he was an effective surgeon because of his ability to turn all his mental energy to a single task. He would not allow himself to be distracted. Whatever he felt about Nati being here was not more important than his father, who was so frail, he looked like he could disappear into a wisp of smoke.

A pressure on his arm forced him to look back. Nati stood, golden curls pulled tight, drawn features from an exhaustion with which he was all too familiar tugging at the edges of her light brown eyes. He very nearly sucked in his breath at how close she stood, all warmth and caramel sweetness.

"Normally, only one of you can be here, but I asked the head nurse to let you be together with him for a little while."

Leo hadn't thought about the logistics of being here with his father. "That's kind of you."

Nati gave a curt nod. Her gaze lingered, an entire conversation in her eyes that he could no longer interpret. They'd once been uncannily attuned to each other, able to communicate with next to no gestures or words, but now, it was like seeing a stranger.

"It's what we do, right? Good night, Leo," Nati said, nodding quickly at his mother and waving to Genevieve. Nati gave him one last searching look before leaving the room, shutting the door quietly behind her.

Tension seemed to bleed out of him the moment she was gone. Genevieve was rummaging through the bag she'd prepared for their father, while his mother was rereading the chart again, as if doing that would reveal an overlooked secret that might make his father get better sooner.

"May I remind you that she saved his life," Genevieve said in a hushed voice, sitting on the edge of the mattress next to Papá and patting his leg softly. "His heart stopped, and she was part of the code team that brought him back."

"She did her job. It's what any doctor worth their salt would have done," Mamá said, setting down the chart she'd been scrutinizing.

"So, she's a doctor worth her salt?" Genevieve shook her head. "It just feels so shabby to let her go like that without acknowledging that fact."

Leo looked at his sister, so young and pretty. It was hard to be Genevieve Espinoza in a family of doctors. She was a writer, not a medical professional. She didn't have interest in the plumbing of the human body that he and his parents had. But she had a generous heart and understood people better than anyone he knew.

"I thanked her when I last spoke to her. Does that help make you feel better, Pluma?"

Genevieve's lovely pale face brightened. "You haven't called me that in years."

"Bet you were missing it," Leo teased.

"Now I do. Not when I was younger. There's nothing like your friends finding out your brother is calling you *quill* and having to hear them tease you about it forever."

"It's a nice nickname!" Leo retorted. "It wasn't even gross or anything."

"It was annoying." Genevieve snorted with laughter before his mother shushed them both.

"Your father needs his rest. Go be silly outside."

Guilt snaked through Leo. Mamá was right. But it was also fair to have such moments with his sister, the person he was the closest to. She'd come regularly to California to visit while Mamá had still worked and run after their father. Genevieve had been kind to Michelle, had visited the hospital where Leo worked and provided an important connection between his life on the West Coast and his family in the East.

She'd kept him abreast of Nati's life, though he had never actually asked her to do so. She'd just known he would want to know.

He'd thought of Nati all these years, often imagining an alternate reality where they were together, either in East Ward or in California. Two doctors doing the things they'd always dreamed of, like opening a neighborhood clinic, or traveling with an organization to lend medical aid in needy places around the world. Then he would come to his senses, force himself to acknowledge reality. There was a time when the possibility of being without her was so absurd, he experienced a total failure of the imagination. Yet here he was, years and years later, doing what he'd once believed impossible—living without Nati. Seeing her again reminded Leo of how not-together he was, that maybe he wasn't doing as well as he thought after all.

Chapter Three

Nati

Nati tapped the tip of her pen on the conference room table of East Ward's Metropolitan Health Alliance, the free clinic she'd cofounded with her best friends, Drs. Caleb Carter and Tahira Hadid. The sound soothed her. She listened to Caleb and Tahira discuss their upcoming presentation and couldn't help but scan the room and try to see it from the point of view of the grant committee. The walls were a soothing turquoise blue, the table a tasteful but simple cherry wood and the upholstered chairs coordinated to the color of the walls.

She'd come home from her shift in the morning, trying and failing to get some sleep before attending this afternoon's meeting. Loiza, her cat, hadn't helped, waking up repeatedly in search of attention. A visual of her fluffy, mildly ferocious tabby came to mind, chasing the red dot around the floor of her tiny apartment, and Nati couldn't help but smile at the thought of her prickly cat at play despite Nati wanting nothing more than to sleep. Her brother, Rafi, couldn't stand Loiza and would have suggested, as usual, all kinds of ways that Nati could free herself of her. She was sure Loiza understood the things he said, judging from the way she growled at him each time he visited.

Between her cat, the shock of treating Leo's father and seeing Leo himself, Nati hadn't been able to sleep deeply. Now, she teetered on the edge of total exhaustion.

Tahira covered Nati's pen to stop her maniacal tapping. When Nati looked up, Caleb and Tahira came into focus, concern reflected on both their faces.

"Are you okay?" Tahira asked.

Nati straightened in her chair. "Yeah." She pushed her curls away from her face—to no avail, as they sprang back again. "Just a lot to do in advance of the committee visits."

In fact, if things went well with their upcoming presentation, their free clinic could be awarded a grant that would overcome several financial obstacles at once. They'd finally be able to afford new community health initiatives that they currently couldn't pay for no matter how much they fundraised. Nati got almost light-headed each time she thought about how much good that money could do in her community.

"None of those nerves have to do with Leo, right?"

Caleb said. "You're not fooling me. I was there when they brought his father in last night."

Tahira perked up, her round, olive-brown face framed by a multicolored headscarf that matched the knee-length violet shirtdress she wore under her lab coat. "Ahem, details please. Do you mean *our* Leo? The Leo who abandoned us?"

Nati groaned. She hadn't mentioned Leo in the hopes that Caleb might catch a clue and not mention him either. She should have known that Caleb would not be able to keep Leo's return to East Ward a secret.

"One and the same." Nati leaned back in her chair, fixing a smile on her face. She didn't want to talk about Leo, but they weren't going to let her get away with that. She gave Tahira a similar summary to the one she'd given Caleb the night before, though she was careful not to give too much away about Leo's father's diagnosis. That was his story to tell.

"How long has it been? Five years?" Tahira asked.

"Six," Nati corrected.

"Those were the days, weren't they?" Caleb said, chuckling under his breath. "I was trying to fit top surgery and recovery between graduating med school and starting my residency in Boston. As if that wasn't going to be some superhuman feat."

"Overachievers are gonna overachieve, right, boo?" Tahira interjected, elbowing Caleb.

"And you," Nati said, directing her comments to Tahira, hoping to keep the subject of conversation away from Leo. "You were sidestepping yet another attempt at an arranged marriage set up by your parents, and ended up marrying the groom-to-be's brother instead."

Tahira rolled her eyes, chuckling to herself. "One marriage and two fur babies later. I'd like to think I got it right in the end."

Caleb laughed as well. "I wouldn't have said no to that either. Kashan is a catch." Tahira's family was from India and had tried to tempt her with a few marriage candidates of their own choosing until Kashan appeared and put an end to all their best-laid plans.

"Yes, he is worth the scandal," Tahira laughed.

"And me," Nati sighed. "I was just trying to get through those last exams and survive my sister planning this ridiculously huge graduation party."

"Please," Caleb said. "You've never met a party you didn't love."

"Guilty!" Nati had always loved doing her life's work during the day and attending banger parties and dancing well into the night. The total opposite of her older brother and sister, although as she moved through her thirties, the parties became shorter and less frequent, replaced with dinners and outings that involved less alcohol and physical exertion than they used to. "Yeah, but it's different when the family gets involved. Getting past that was…a moment."

"And all the things that happened between you and Leo," Tahira added.

"Yeah," Nati said quietly. They didn't know all the details of what had happened between them, only that she'd broken things off all the while behaving as if it didn't matter, when in reality, her relationship with

Leo was one of the things that had made her the most happy. She found herself tapping the desk with her pen again, but a pointed look from Tahira prompted her to stop.

"That's all water under the bridge, right?" Tahira asked.

Nati breathed deeply, exercising her usual control over her nerves, an automatic smile unfurling over her face again. That's how she dealt with things. Humor. Fortitude. She put others at ease to keep them from seeing her own distress. As the youngest of the three Navarro siblings, she was the one everyone had rallied around when their mother died. Being the center of that intense attention had taught Nati early on to suppress anything that might cause her family any more worry.

But Caleb and Tahira knew her too well to let her get away with lying to them—or herself.

Nati waved her hand as if brushing aside an insect. "Totally. All in the past."

"Is it, though?" Tahira prodded. "Because it doesn't seem like those waters are very peaceful."

"Totally peaceful. Not a wave in sight," Nati said, giving them her best and brightest smile.

"Well, it's not water under the bridge for me," Tahira huffed, crossing her arms, giving both Caleb and Nati a pointed look. "He just abandoned us. Didn't bother to keep in touch, even though we had been best friends for so long."

"That was my fault," Nati said, the tapping getting faster. "Remember, I'm the one who broke up with him. He probably doesn't ever want to lay eyes on me again."

This time, it was Caleb's turn to stop her pen. "I can't speak to what happened between the two of you. But he's the one who decided that breaking up with you meant breaking up with us. That's on him. We loved you as a couple, but we love you individually as well."

Tahira huffed. "Honestly, I've always loved Nati a little more than I loved him."

"Stop it," Nati said around a laugh, while underneath the teasing and banter, all she wanted to do was put her head down on the table and rest. Yes, she'd broken up with Leo. Yes, she'd made him believe that her feelings weren't strong enough to weather a long-distance relationship. But she'd done it for the right reasons. If she didn't believe that, she would make herself sick thinking about what she'd willfully thrown away.

And anyway, if he'd gone and gotten married so soon after their breakup, maybe her decision to end things hadn't been such a mistake after all.

Nati decided to get things back on track. "About the shadowing requirement. I'm looking at your schedules, and it doesn't seem like either of you have a whole lot more time to give."

"I can spare one additional day this month," Tahira said. Her work as a trauma surgeon kept her busy. "I've already set my schedule at the hospital, and only mortal illness will get me to change it."

Nati groaned. "Caleb?"

He sighed, smoothing down his coat. "I can work around a few things, but it's a little tight for me, too."

"Great." Nati leaned back, bumping her head against the leather chair. "Guess it's going to be me. Karma decided to take a big bite out of my ass."

"Classy, Nati," Tahira laughed.

"I mean, it is a pretty big ass, sis," Caleb chimed in.

Nati made a show of looking back over her shoulder. "No junk shaming allowed. This is a grade-A prime Puerto Rican ass. Not surprised that karma came for it."

"No surprise when anyone comes for it," Tahira giggled. "Okay, so will you email the schedule to the committee?"

"Yeah, seeing as most of these suggested dates are mine," Nati answered with resignation. No reason for Tahira or Caleb to know just how twisted up she was over Leo's sudden reappearance in her life. She'd ended things with him. It was no one's fault that he was able to get over her so quickly. And hardly his fault that it had taken her forever to do the same. That maybe she still wasn't quite over him.

The past needed to stay where it belonged. She had too many important things going on to trifle with throwbacks to the life she didn't get to live.

Caleb and Tahira left her in the conference room to type out the email. She reread it for errors, making sure to purge it of everything but the most professional language, and double-checked each email address as it loaded from her contacts.

She sighed, hitting Send, her thoughts of Leo spinning on endless repeat in her head.

Momentary relief from her thoughts came when her phone vibrated with a reminder. She was in the habit of setting notifications with a voice-to-text component for appointments as soon as she made them, reviewing them each morning before she started her day. Given the events of the last several hours, she was especially grateful for the reminder that she was supposed to pick up a few things for dinner with the entire Navarro family the next day. She had completely forgotten, and now she couldn't find it in her to follow through on the errand.

Today was turning into a lot.

Leo's face appeared in her thoughts as she had seen him that afternoon—a bit older, a bit more rugged and so handsome, it was like a hand had reached into her body to squeeze the last beats of her heart. She rubbed her chest, as if massaging her lungs would get rid of the tightness that kept her from catching her breath. She almost smiled in reaction to the stress, but she was alone and could drop the facade. There was no one here to pretend for.

She gave herself permission to feel all the things she rarely acknowledged publicly—shock, pain, regret and a hefty side of self-loathing. Each emotion drilled through her uninterrupted, forcing Nati to recognize that, after all these years, she was still struggling to put aside an ex who had meant so much to her when they were together yet who had found it so easy to replace her.

She couldn't let her family know anything was up—they often forgot that she wasn't a little girl any longer. She was an adult and would do what she always did: put on her game face and pretend everything was going perfectly. There was no room for these negative feelings with them. That wasn't the version of Nati she served up. She was going to be light as a breeze and happy as sunshine, shoving down anything that would dampen that brightness. If she was lucky, she would have very little to do with Leo once his father was discharged, and things would get easier. She might even stop thinking of him every moment of her day.

Shutting her laptop with more force than necessary, she gathered up her things and headed for her shift at the ER.

Chapter Four

Leo

His father woke up sometime before dawn. Leo, who had sent his mother and sister home to let them get some sleep, felt like he could finally breathe again.

"Papá," he whispered as the nurse checked his father's vitals.

His father blinked several times, gave him a small smile behind the oxygen mask, then scanned the room, as if searching for someone.

"Mamá was here, but she went home with Genevieve," Leo said, rightly guessing his curiosity. "They were here the whole night and needed sleep."

"*Y tú?*" his father rasped. Leo looked to the nurse for permission to remove the mask, which she gave. He lifted it carefully from his father's face.

"I'm used to not getting much sleep," answered Leo. "It's part of the job. You should know that."

Papá gave a small huff of laughter that sputtered out at the end. "My throat is dry."

Anticipating this need, the nurse had placed a cup of ice on the tray next to his father's bed. Leo picked it up and gently slid one chip after another past his father's cracked lips, leaving droplets that Leo had to wipe away using the tissue provided. It was slow and painstaking work, as if his father were becoming accustomed to the use of his mouth again.

Leo had grown up with an image of his father as a heroic figure. His father had been a top student in medical school and had later occupied positions of prestige before his defection, managing to rebuild a life all over again in the US almost from scratch. It was one of the most often-told stories in his family, to the extent that it had become a family legend. To see him so frail and diminished fragmented something in Leo, and he had to turn away on the pretext of washing his hands to keep his father from seeing the tears that were too close to spilling out. He couldn't do that. He did not have the luxury of a breakdown.

The door of the room clicked open. Leo dried his hands with a paper towel and turned to find Nati, hair tied back, crisp white coat over a pair of black slacks and a ginger-colored button-down that complemented her natural bronze coloring. A gold chain glittered around the long column of her neck, smooth and unblemished as the rest of her skin. Nati had very few birthmarks. He knew. He'd once set out to count them.

"Coming to check on Raul. The nurse told me he was awake," Nati said quietly, lifting the chart and scanning it as she approached the bed.

"He felt thirsty, so I gave him ice," Leo said, a little uselessly. He was trained to do more, but his expertise was all knotted up with stress and worry over his father's condition.

"I trust your professional judgment." Nati flicked a glance to where Leo stood before fixing her gaze on his father, who had shut his eyes after the strain of accepting ice chips. She checked his IV and other tubes, working quietly and efficiently. Papá opened his eyes and gazed at her. Leo approached, setting a hand on his father's to let him know he wasn't alone.

"Nati?" came Raul's breathless voice.

Nati smiled down at Papá. "*Hola*, Señor Espinoza."

"Ay, *mija*," he said, smiling at her. "*Que bueno verte despues de tantos años.*"

"*Igual*," Nati said, her face crinkling into that familiar smile that still managed to send starbursts of excitement through Leo's chest. "But if you wanted to visit me, you didn't have to have a cardiac event to do so."

"*Verdad*, because you are working here. Genevieve told me at one point." He breathed heavily, as if that was all the oxygen he could spare in speaking to her.

Nati brushed his thinning hair off his forehead. "You gave everyone a scare, you know that?"

Papá gave another one of those small huffs that passed as laughter. "I gave myself a scare."

Nati patted his hand. "*Tranquilo.* We'll talk when you feel better. I'm just glad to see you awake. If you get better and your tests come back clean, you might even be able to go home by the end of the week."

"Gracias, hija mia," he whispered before his eyes fluttered shut and he drifted off to unconsciousness again.

My daughter. She could have been. Once upon a time.

Leo schooled his face to hide the stab of pain that speared through him.

Nati stared at Papá for a few beats before inhaling noisily, shoving a hand in her pocket. She didn't look at Leo. "He's not much older than my father."

Leo thought of Enrique, an elegant, thin man with the kind of energy that made him appear electric. Every emotion Leo had been suppressing rose up to form a lump in his throat, desperate for release. The stress of his father's hospitalization, the weight of memory and longing caused by Nati's presence and his own exhaustion were getting to him. He had to stay cool. "How is Enrique?"

Nati lifted her eyes to his, pursing her lips together. In another life, he would have smoothed the pucker of those lips with a kiss of his own. "Stubborn as always. Won't consider retiring or cutting back at the restaurant. I worry about him sometimes."

"It takes a lot to convince these old-school men that they might not be able to do the things they once did." He thought of his own father, trying to do everything before the cancer had weakened him. He cast around for a subject change. "I heard Rafi got married. And Val, too."

Nati perked up at this. She had always been close to her siblings. "I have pictures." She took out her phone to show him wedding pictures of both Val and Rafi with their respective husbands.

Leo smiled at the photos. He remembered Val as tough, sweet and earnest. She'd given him the benefit of the doubt right away, born of her uncomplicated love for her sister and a desire to see her happy. He'd had to work a little harder to win Rafi over to his side, with his diffidence toward new people and typical big-brother overprotectiveness. But once it was clear that Leo had only good intentions toward Nati, Rafi had stopped with the side-eyeing and barely repressed threats of violence if anything happened to his sister. He wasn't a particularly big guy, but he'd always struck Leo as the type who'd find your car and slit the tires, including all the leather inside while he was at it. Leo had thought better of provoking him.

Nati's eyes fell again. This was a version of Nati he hadn't seen often in their time together. She wasn't usually shy about anything, but now she was positively bashful. "If you're in town, you could consider coming to Navarro's and saying hello. My family always did like you."

Leo was taken by surprise. Enrique was such a contrast to his mother. Open-minded, bighearted and full of generosity. He took life as it came without expecting much from it, grateful for whatever it gave him. But that wasn't what had thrown him off his center. "You don't mind me coming to say hello?"

Nati tilted her head to the side, considering him. "Why would I mind that? Unless you mind."

Of course, why would she mind? She was not the one who had gotten broken up with. She wasn't the one who had had her heart ripped out of her chest and stomped on repeatedly. She probably hadn't given Leo a second thought all these years. Visiting her father didn't provoke the turbulence of emotion in her that it did him. If anything, she was most likely indifferent to the whole situation.

"I'll think about it," Leo said, not wanting to sound sullen. But it was hard meeting the great love of your life after so many years and realizing you didn't matter to her the way she did to you.

"Please do." Nati glanced back at Papá, who was in a deep sleep, and sighed. "How long are you in East Ward?"

Leo had so many other things he wanted to say to Nati, none of which had to do with their current topic of conversation. But he didn't know how to put any of it into words. They were just feelings all spooled together like the tangled ties of a pair of scrubs or the knotted elastic of a box of masks.

"I'm not sure. I took a leave of absence. I wanted to help my mother and sister care for him."

Nati's eyes were as wide as saucers and full of emotion. "The worst thing in the world is to look back at the time you could have spent with the people you love and realize those lost moments will never return." Her laugh was short and bitter. "Family matters more than everything."

"You didn't always think that way," Leo said quietly, unable to contain the words and only partly regretting them. He had once been her family as well.

Nati looked like she'd been struck. "And what is that supposed to mean?"

Leo rubbed the space between his eyebrows. What was he saying? "Don't mind me. I'm just exhausted and not making a lot of sense."

The door of the room opened, and Genevieve and Zoraida entered. The look Zoraida gave Nati could scorch the surface of the sun, but Genevieve either didn't notice or didn't care, because she stepped forward to give Nati a giant hug.

"The nurse told us Papá woke up. How is he?" Genevieve asked.

"He wore himself out talking to us, but now he's sleeping again," Leo answered.

Zoraida's face grew dark. "Don't you know better than to exhaust your patient so soon after a code, Dr. Navarro?" Zoraida said Nati's name like a sneer.

Nati lifted her chin, her eyes narrow. "You may file a complaint with the patient liaison if you believe my care has been insufficient or negligent in any way."

Nati turned to Genevieve before Zoraida, whose face had gone white, could respond. "If you need anything else, the nurse on duty can contact me."

Without another word, she turned on her heel and strode out of the room. As soon as the door was closed, Genevieve whirled on her mother. "I said we should thank Nati for all she'd done, not make her feel incompetent."

Zoraida's crossed her arms, her posture stiffening. "I made a simple, clinical observation."

"You were unnecessarily rude, like you've always been with her. She saved Papá's life. Do you want to get that through your head?" Genevieve shoved the overnight bag she'd brought with her onto one of the bland-colored armchairs in the room.

Zoraida pushed a lock of hair behind her ear. With rest and time, she had made herself up, her jeans and silk blouse impeccable. "You say I'm unnecessarily rude, but she ended up breaking your brother's heart, so perhaps I wasn't so wrong about her after all."

"You weren't rude to her because of Leo. You were rude because you can't stand her! Don't gaslight me," Genevieve retorted.

"Forget it, Pluma. She's already rewritten history to suit her own narrative," Leo said to his sister, rubbing his face as if he could wipe away the exhaustion.

This day had gone on long enough. "Papá is doing fine," Leo said to his mother, whose face had turned to stone in her anger. "You're good to take a cab home tonight, Ma?"

Zoraida shrugged, her frown fierce. "I do it all the time."

"Leo," Genevieve said, but Leo was already out the door.

As he boarded the dingy train in the direction of his sister's place, he reflected on his mother's behavior. She thought few people were good enough for her children, not because of who he and Genevieve were, but because this was part of the very specific vision for how her family should look. His ex-wife, Michelle, the daughter of an important surgeon at an important metropolitan hospital, was the kind of woman she had in mind for her son, but Leo's marriage had been a spectacularly bad idea between two people who were better off as friends. Nati's family did not have those kinds of connections, and she was therefore instantly disqualified. In his mother's mind, Nati's breaking up with Leo had changed from a welcome outcome to yet another justification for disliking her, further confirmation of her opinion of Nati.

When Leo arrived at the apartment, he set his things inside and went directly to the bar Genevieve kept well stocked to mix himself a mojito. He'd taken a bartending course for the hell of it the summer he'd turned twenty-one, instantly making him popular at college parties. But it was also relaxing to indulge when he had a minute to breathe from his schoolwork. It was one of the things he'd loved to do when he went out with Nati—go to his friends' houses and be the designated bartender for a few hours. Nati had once partied as hard as she worked and never turned down a chance to socialize if her workload permitted it, a quality they both shared. Leo loved people; he loved going out and having a good time.

He took a sip of his concoction, the cool, crisp mint a soothing balm to a day that had been full of too many emotional peaks to climb.

He rubbed his face before walking to the wall-to-wall window of his apartment, catching sight of the dark river that flowed below. A riverside apartment in

Wagner Waterfront Place was a pure indulgence—his sister could have rented something humbler, he supposed, but like Leo, Genevieve liked beauty and good things. He was one hundred percent aware of the fact that, having been raised in an affluent family by parents who gave an incredible amount of importance to appearance and fashion, not only the tendency but also the means to be a show-off would rub off on them as well. His father, who collected art, jewelry and cars, had influenced this particular weakness in them both. The way Leo saw it, his father had paid his dues in life struggles and his mother had worked her ass off, both looking for success in this country. They were entitled to enjoy the fruits of their labors, or there was no point in making so many sacrifices.

He thought back to his time with Nati, how much he'd enjoyed giving gifts to her. He'd plied Nati with jewelry, clothes and especially shoes, which she loved. She'd always fussed at him not to do so. She couldn't afford those things herself, yet pride did not make her an easy one to give things to. But that didn't stop him. One gift in particular, a beautiful necklace with a diamond set in pearl, had stood out to him. It had looked like melted gold against her skin, and he'd made love to her while she wore it, one of his most vivid memories of their time together. His body stirred at the thought of the gold chain caressing her velvet skin. He wondered if she still owned it. He wondered if she had kept anything he'd given her.

Nati might have broken his heart, but he hadn't been able to let the mementos of their time together disappear into oblivion. He still had the gifts she'd given him. A rare mixed-drink recipe book that included a history of spirits. A timepiece for a vest he'd never wear, simply because he'd admired a similar one when they were binge-watching *Doctor Who* one cold winter weekend. The little sticky notes with messages written out in ink from the pens she loved so much, even though handwriting was such a chore for her sometimes. A book of poetry, a surprising gift from someone as pragmatic as she was. Carnival tokens, plastic necklaces, *Phineas and Ferb* fan art. All those souvenirs from their time together, the years their lives had intersected, echoes of an old and now defunct hope that they would share many more.

He rolled his head, stretching out the kinks in his neck. He needed to be thinking about his father and next steps to help him in his treatment and, hopefully, recovery. Why the hell couldn't his brain just quit its obsession with thinking of her? He stared out the windows over the now darkening river, as if the cool currents of the Hudson might give him the answers he sought.

Chapter Five

Nati

After her shift, Nati stopped off at home to feed Loiza and pet her so she wouldn't be too upset that Nati was coming home later than usual. Sometimes, Papi would do her the favor of keeping Loiza company when Nati was gone, but Papi was downstairs at Navarro's Family Restaurant, getting things ready for their family dinner. Her head was still full from her run-in with Leo. Every time she saw him, he dredged up more and more memories, a thousand moments she thought she'd buried away. The first time she'd seen him across the biochemistry lecture hall, head bent over his computer, taking the same notes Nati had recorded so she could transcribe them after. Echoes of emotions, bits of images, smells and tastes that still lived in her body, tormenting her with his presence.

She walked faster, hoping the effort would dispel her feelings.

She arrived at the door of her family's building, the restaurant already closed for the afternoon, and wound her way through the main hallway to access the restaurant from an internal door.

She thought of her residency days, after things had ended with Leo. How hard she'd worked to keep herself from thinking of Leo's absence, of the void she had created. How her insomnia had frequently driven her to stop in the restaurant to help Val and their father until exhaustion quieted her brain and she could dare to sleep without the fear of Leo invading her thoughts. It was a fool move, because while her waking brain could be deceived by overwork to keep him hidden from her thoughts, her dreams were out of her control and more than made up for the lack of Leo in her daytime thoughts.

Nati stopped at the threshold of the kitchen and closed her eyes. She couldn't meet her family in this state and give them a reason to worry about her. She needed to pull herself together, harness every last bit of energy to put on her best face. She had always kept her struggles to herself, and today was not the day to change that.

Once she'd achieved some kind of equilibrium, she fixed her usual smile on her face and entered the restaurant. Navarro's was normally immaculate when closed; this evening, there were signs of food preparations, like steaming metal pots with the telltale aroma of Caribbean spices—bay leaves, sazón and her brother-in-law's epis. Nati, whose food curiosity was embedded deep in her blood, lifted the lids and was thrilled to see a veritable feast of Haitian rice and beans, Puerto Rican stewed beef with carrots and potatoes, chicken francese thanks to Val's husband and all the sides that one would expect from a family dinner where diet and good health had been tossed to the wind. This, despite what the doctor had said to Papi about his elevated blood pressure.

With a suddenly rumbling stomach, Nati followed the sounds of conversation from the dining area that filtered over the hiss of simmering pots.

"Maybe this is what you need to finally consider retirement." Her brother's voice cut across from the kitchen.

Nati popped her head around the kitchen door in time to see Papi, normally flawless in appearance, even in his work clothes, sitting with eyes red-rimmed and curly hair in disarray. Seated with him at the table was her brother, Rafi, and his husband, Étienne. Panic seized Nati at the evidence that her father was in distress, and she dispensed with the usual pleasantries. "What's going on? Why is Papi crying?"

Rafi, who resembled their father to an uncanny degree with his curly, dark brown hair, dusky olive skin and enormous brown eyes, blinked at Nati, slowly registering her presence. Quicker with the human interaction part, Étienne was on his feet, bending to hug her in greeting.

"Ma petite." He said his nickname for her with un-

characteristic emotion in his Haitian accent. "It is so good to see you."

Her brother-in-law's gentle greeting went some way toward mollifying her, though something still felt off. "Hello, *cuñado*." Nati kissed his cheek. "What's happening?"

"So much!" Rafi blurted out before Étienne could answer, biting off the rest of his words. He was a high school math teacher and normally a competent communicator, which meant something was really up if he was thrown off balance so badly. Rafi stood to accept his sister's kiss before she released him to kneel next to her father, who was still seated, and deliver a kiss in greeting. "*Estás bien, mi viejo?*"

Papi's gave her a dazed, watery smile. "*Sí, sí.* Really good, actually." Nati handed him a napkin, which he used to blot tears from his eyes. "Why don't you help your brother put out the plates?" He indicated with a jut of his chin at the tables that had been dragged in a row so the entire family could sit together.

"Papi," Nati began to protest, but he put up a hand. "*Paciencia, mija.* Let's prepare everything, first. You'll find out soon enough."

Nati wanted to shake her father until he told her what was happening, but obeying him was too ingrained a habit. So she did as she was told, even if the curiosity was eating her alive. She cast a questioning look at her brother, who was chewing his lip, a flush spreading beneath his dark cheeks.

"Come on, big brother, you know you want to tell me what's up," Nati cooed.

Rafi's face wrinkled into the biggest grin she'd ever seen. "Don't you start that, Nati. You know I have zero self-control."

"I know. That's why I'm asking, favorite brother of mine." She batted her eyes, then gave him a dramatic pout. "Ay, don't make your baby sister suffer."

"You are such a pest!" Rafi exclaimed, his skin shiny and pink. He looked up at Étienne as if asking for permission. Étienne simply shrugged, a giant grin on his face as well. "Who am I to tell you what to do, *zanj mwen*?" Étienne wrapped Rafi up in a one-armed hug that Rafi melted into and directed his comments to Nati. "We wanted to tell everyone at the same time, but Rafi is about to burst like a balloon."

"I am. *¡Me voy a reventar!*" Rafi exclaimed.

"So dramatic," Nati giggled, glancing at her father, who was grinning as he placed a water carafe on the table before glaring at her brother. "Well? Out with it!"

He moaned as if whatever he was keeping to himself was eating its way out of him. "Okay, fine. Nicola, Étienne and I went to the doctor today, and she's passed the twelve-week mark." Rafi's cheeks were going to catch fire any moment now. Étienne squeezed him close, unable to stop grinning. Papi wiped his face of new tears, smiling into his hand.

"Nicola is pregnant?" Nati said, jumping to her feet. "And you waited three months to tell us?"

"We didn't want to jinx it. Twelve weeks is one of the most important milestones." Rafi nodded excitedly. "Every month that passes means we have a better chance—"

"—of having a baby," Étienne finished for him.

"Oh, my God, congratulations, you guys!" Nati shouted, throwing her arms around Rafi and Étienne in the most inelegant way possible, banging into the table and nearly knocking over the full carafe Papi had just set there. Papi yelped but managed to scoop it out of the way before she overturned it completely. Nicola, one of Étienne's closest friends, had agreed to be a surrogate for their child. For the briefest moment, a conversation with Leo from many years ago came back to her in which they'd discussed marriage as a hypothetical, where they would hold the ceremony and go for their honeymoon. They'd also discussed how they would organize their lives if they had children so neither had to set their career aside while growing a family. Nati tried to clear her head. It was only because she'd just seen him—no other reason for her sudden trip down memory lane.

Squealing and clapping, Nati grasped at the joy she felt at her brother's news and held onto it. She threw her arms around her father, putting the table closest to them in danger of Nati's hips again. "Does Val know yet?"

"Does Val know what?"

Nati turned to see her big sister approach from the door Nati had entered earlier, looking gorgeous and happy, her normally curly dark brown hair blown out straight and framing her huge dark eyes and pretty brown face. She wore jeans and a pink off-the-shoulder sweater that would have looked sloppy on anyone else but on her and paired with adorable pink boots, made her seem hip. Philip, a tall white man who was more cinnamon bun than actual person, brought up the rear.

The back door shut, then opened again as their cousin, Olivia, nearly smashed into Philip's back, all bold black makeup and pale skin, lips painted bloodred to match the dark aesthetic of her clothes.

"Hey, pretty boy, watch out," she snapped, though there was no bite in her comment. Philip rolled his eyes but let her step ahead of him. Olivia's verbal haranguing was part of the backdrop of their collective lives and was as expected as the sunset. "What's the emergency?" Olivia demanded as she dropped her bag on the back of a chair.

"Why would you think there's an emergency? It's just a family dinner," Rafi exclaimed, but the look on Papi's face was practically a declaration of guilt. Étienne rubbed the pressure point between his eyebrows, unable to suppress a grin.

"Papi sent a message to come early. He said it was an emergency," Val said.

"Now we know where the siblings come by their love of the dramatic." Étienne placed a hand on Papi's shoulder, smiling indulgently.

"I'm innocent of all wrongdoing," Papi said, the smile on his face anything but innocent.

"Never a dull moment with them," Philip said, acknowledging Rafi and Papi with a wave now that the previously empty dining room felt perfectly full, crowded with the people Nati loved the most. Nati bit her hand to keep from bursting with the joy of what she knew. If Rafi didn't say something soon, she was going to climb upstairs to her apartment and shout out the news from the fire escape for the whole neighborhood to hear.

Rafi, flushing from the embarrassment of everyone's attention on him, answered, "Okay, okay. It's not an emergency. It's…good news." He gazed at Étienne, his face full of love and reverence. "We came directly from the clinic and, well, we're going to be dads."

Val and Olivia looked at each other, eyes swinging toward Nati then back at Rafi and Étienne before erupting into shouts of excitement, nearly knocking Rafi and Étienne on their backs as they crowded them with what seemed like bodies that had sprouted several extra sets of arms.

"Of course, you couldn't hold news like that to yourselves," Philip said, his reactions always low-key but sincere, eyes overbrimming as Étienne extricated himself from the knot of Val and Olivia's arms to hug his friend, squeezing him tight. "I'm so happy for you."

"It has been a journey," Étienne agreed. They'd been trying for the past year, and the in vitro costs had been ridiculous, especially when Nicola hadn't become pregnant right away. "But it's something we've wanted since the very beginning." His eyes found Rafi, who encouraged him with a gaze that spoke volumes.

Val came up beside Philip, who placed an arm around her and squeezed. "We're going to be *titis*," Val said with a kind of breathless wonder.

"That is going to be one spoiled baby, cuz," Olivia said, crushing Rafi in a hug.

Nati sighed, satisfied. She couldn't believe that both her brother and sister, who she always visualized with their funny-print pajamas and wild, unkempt hair, tumbling over each other as they jockeyed for control of the television on Sunday mornings, were married adults, starting businesses and having children of their own. Even Olivia, who flew under everyone's radar with her ultra-independent ways, was building her own business that had corporations outside of East Ward taking notice.

Everyone was moving ahead. Time passed and things inevitably changed. The past wasn't a place where anyone wanted to live, no matter how compelling it might be. Nati's thoughts wandered back to Leo. He was always one unexpected reminder away from being at the forefront of her mind, even with the span of years between them. But now? After showing up in her life, feeding her starved imagination with new images of him, a little older, a little bit more handsome, a whole lot more compelling? He was taking up residence in her brain like a squatter, refusing to leave. This was not how she wanted to live. She needed to be like her family, all of whom were finding ways to move forward, not slipping back into the tired habits and disappointments of the past.

Watching her family's happy faces, Nati was saddened that her mother was not here to witness the evolution of her children's lives. It was so unfair that the one person besides her father who would have found so much joy in the current state of the Navarro family would be the one person who couldn't be present. Nati had to squash a sudden, familiar surge of choking rage at the absence of her mother, a feeling that, even after all these years, she found hard to quell. She wouldn't give way to that, not here. She would never let her family see that part of her.

"We have champagne," Papi said, pulling out an impressively expensive bottle of Pierre-Jouët's Belle Époque from beneath the mini sink at the sandwich counter. "I've been saving this for a special occasion. I think a toast to my first grandchild is the best way to drink it."

Nati fixed a smile on her face as Rafi came to stand next to Papi behind the counter. "Papi," he said, taking the bottle of champagne in hand, "What are you doing, hiding two-hundred-dollar bottles of Pierre-Jouët under the service counter sink?"

"It's cool enough there for them to keep," Papi shrugged, setting down champagne glasses he'd fetched from the back.

"Them? You have more than one down there, of all places?" Val stared at him in horror, and even Philip had an eyebrow raised in surprise. "That's not where you keep champagne like that, *Dios mío*."

"It's probably better if we just open the bottles and rescue them from the depths of your kitchen cabinet hell," Olivia said, snatching the bottle from Rafi and pointing it towards the ceiling.

"Hey, it's my kid we're celebrating!" Rafi complained.

"Too bad, pumpkin. I'm the *titi* and I say we all get smashed."

"Olivia!" came the collective groan from everyone present.

* * *

Nati rested the back of her head on the cool windowpane, legs stretched out on the cushion of the booth. The champagne had gone down as smooth as its price suggested. Nati was mellow, head lolling against the glass, thoughts of the day meandering in and out of her mind like lazy shadows on concrete, and she let them. After an emotional couple of days, she was entitled to a little relaxation. Val and Philip had been the first to leave, begging off with the (legitimate) excuse that they had too much left to do with the second restaurant's grand opening just around the corner. Rafi and Étienne soon followed, no doubt exhausted from the excitement of their good news and the dinner they'd prepared. Papi was already upstairs, so it was just Nati and her cousin, Olivia, who was sprawled in a similar position opposite from her in the booth, a bottle of champagne and two flutes sitting between them.

Nati did a good job of keeping her feelings under lock and key with her family. But her brain was still reliving Leo's arrival into her life again like a film reel playing on loop in her brain. The champagne made her more inclined to talk about it with Olivia, who lived for other people's drama and was going through something of her own.

"She said she had to go to Florida to take care of her mom. And I totally respect that," Olivia was saying. "But why does that have to be the end of us?"

"Maybe Aleysha didn't have the emotional bandwidth to deal with a long-distance relationship as well as care for her mother. It's a lot and something was going to have to give. She probably realized that something would be you," Nati said, her thoughts wheeling back to Leo again. Nati had broken things off with his best interests at heart. And even if it stung, she had no right to wonder why he'd gone and married someone else so soon after. She'd chosen that path for them and had convinced herself that she'd learned to live with it. "So instead of putting you through that, she broke up with you."

"But I would have worked with her, Nati," Olivia dropped her feet onto the floor, slouching as she poured more champagne into her glass. "She didn't have a right to make that kind of decision for the both of us. A relationship means teamwork. And she was not thinking team Oleysha."

Nati nearly choked on her champagne. "Girl, please, that can't be your ship name. It sounds like a brand of face cream."

Olivia's nearly pitch-black eyes widened until they seemed to cover half her face. "My heart is completely annihilated here and you're picking on my ship name? You're cold."

"If you want flattery, hit Étienne up. He'll take care of you," Nati retorted. "You're staying with me tonight, right? Don't think I'm going to let you go home in this condition."

Olivia shrugged, her straight black hair hanging over her forehead as if she hadn't seen the business end of a brush in days. Nati leaned forward and moved a cluster of hair out of the way as Olivia answered, "I'm not drunk."

Nati reached over the table and snatched Olivia's

purse, wedging it between her body and the leather seat. "You're. Staying. With. Me."

"Fine, *caramba*. Least you can do after making fun of me," Oliva huffed, growing more serious. "I hate that she made this decision for the both of us without talking to me about it. She just gave me back my apartment key and left. As if the last four years hadn't meant anything to her."

Nati squirmed, blaming her discomfort on the leather purse poking into her thigh. "Aleysha seemed really in love with you, if that means anything."

"No, it actually makes me feel worse. Just a reminder of what we're both missing out on." Olivia rubbed her forehead, taking a sip from her glass. "Tell me something to distract me. Did you rescue a toy from someone's intestine? Cut open someone's chest cavity to massage their heart? Please—anything." Olivia bit a trembling lip, shaking her head as if forcing a fly to take off. "I'm struggling here."

"Aww, baby." Nati got out of her seat and slid in next to her cousin, hugging her close. Olivia was about the same age as Val, and she had spent so much time with the Navarro siblings growing up, she might as well be a sister to all of them, especially with her mother living all the way in Puerto Rico. It was inconceivable to hold any kind of family event and not invite Olivia. "I'm so sorry." After Nati had relaxed her grip, she sat up, squaring her shoulders. "As it happens, I do have something to share."

"Finally," Olivia said, wiping the tears from her cheeks.

She yanked several napkins from the dispenser and blew her nose. "You know I live for other people's drama."

Nati gave Olivia a quick squeeze. "Okay, so at work the other night, a patient came through undergoing a cardiac event."

"English, please," Olivia said.

"Sorry. Just means that the patient's heart stopped."

Olivia's face softened, a crease appearing between her eyebrows. "I'm sorry, Nati. You deal with life and death stuff all day, and here I am, crying all over you because my longtime girlfriend broke up with me."

"Don't apologize for being heartbroken. We're supposed to show up for each other."

Olivia smiled softly, an expression she almost never wore. Tenderness for her unhinged, eccentric cousin washed over Nati. "So, what happened?"

Nati spread her hands, looking at her nail gloss and the extra-dry skin, a consequence of the constant handwashing and disinfecting she did as part of her profession. "We saved the man."

Olivia took another sip of her champagne, studying Nati the way she did when she was trying to figure out what someone was trying to hide from her. "Okay."

"That's not the gossip, though." Nati steadied her breathing. Even thinking back on it flipped her insides. "Guess who the patient was?"

Olivia shook her head, pure confusion written across her face. "I have no idea."

Nati smiled, but then she felt the smile vanish. Maybe it was the champagne or the sheer emotional exhaustion, but she couldn't muster a mask for this one. "Leo Espinoza's father."

Olivia's face turned into one giant *O*. "*The* Leo Espinoza. Heartbreak on legs, aka Dr. Sabroso?"

"Don't," Nati said, wagging her finger at her. "Don't start with that nickname."

"Uh, excuse me, Nati 'that-sounds-like-face-cream' Navarro. You owe me for kicking me when I was still down."

"Fine. I earned it," Nati snapped before proceeding to tell Olivia all about stabilizing Raul, her surprise at seeing Leo and his family in the waiting room, her shock at discovering he'd come back to East Ward to help care for his father.

"What I don't understand is how he could show up without warning at least Tahira and Caleb that he was coming?" Nati said, repeating the question she'd been asking in her head a thousand times. "Why did he disappear from everyone's life like that?"

"That doesn't take a medical degree to figure out. Tahira and Caleb are collateral damage from your breakup," Olivia said, wiping at a champagne bubble that clung to her nose with the back of her hand. "Not even joint custody. He got his fancy residency, and you got the besties."

"He could have kept being their friend. He didn't have to cut everyone off." Just Nati. And Nati would have understood.

"Not that easy—not if it meant running the risk of seeing you again. And last time I checked, *you* broke up with *him*." Olivia poured Nati another drink.

"So?" Nati said, Olivia's words scorching through her brain. "I did it for his own good."

"Oh, wonderful. The 'let's-break-people's-hearts-for-their-own-good' plane has just landed. Come on, Nati. It's not that hard to understand. You ended a relationship he wanted, so he cut his losses and left."

"I wanted it, too. Doesn't that count for something?" Nati deflated in her seat. She knew what the answer was. She didn't need her cousin, who was really going through it, to be the one to break it down for her.

"It counts for absolutely nothing. Intentions are worthless. Results are what matter, and the result here is that you broke his heart. That's it. That's the tea."

Nati groaned. Olivia was right. She was always annoyingly, infallibly right. "Hey, tomorrow is Sunday, and I'm off. I only have to go into the clinic and do a little paperwork in the morning. Want to go shopping with me? I can be your bisexual support buddy, if you like."

Olivia narrowed her eyes in consideration. Then, with decisive flair, she threw back her champagne and slapped the table with her free hand, perhaps with a little more force than she intended. "You know what? My broken heart *is* gonna need some retail therapy, right after I get over this hangover. Ugh. Why did we swallow two bottles of champagne again?"

"Because it was free, and the only thing we have to worry about is crawling upstairs to my place."

"Oh, right." Olivia blotted her cheeks with a paper napkin again. "So what are you going to do about Leo?"

Nati shrugged. "There's nothing to do. I mean, once his father is released to his personal physican's care, I won't see him again. And anyway, I'm too busy trying to get funding for the clinic to really think about him or anything else."

"So there's no issue, right? Don't tell me you're not over your ex after all these years."

Nati pressed the heels of her hands into her eyes. "I'm not sure, to be honest. He's married, you know."

Olivia sat up a little straighter in the booth. "What about him? How did he seem to you?"

Nati dropped her hands, blinking the sudden glare of light away. "Gorgeous. Distraught. Indifferent, to me, at least." She shrugged. "I got to see Genevieve, though. We were good friends while I was dating Leo. She treated me the same as always, as if time hadn't passed for any of us." Like Tahira and Caleb for Leo, Genevieve had been one more piece of collateral damage in her breakup with Leo.

Olivia signed, leaning on her hand, her eyes beginning to flutter closed. "You know, I think I'm gonna crash at your place after all."

"That's what I've been saying all this time!" Nati retorted, sliding out of the booth, her legs rubbery as she helped Olivia to her feet. Olivia, who was about Nati's height, slung an arm over her shoulder as if hoping Nati might carry her upstairs.

Except instead of leaning on Nati, Olivia gave her cousin a kiss on the cheek and a squeeze, the only dead weight that of her arm draped across Nati's shoulders. "Thank you, *prima*, for…" Olivia shrugged.

"Listening?" Nati interjected.

Olivia nodded, opening the back door of the restaurant that led into the corridor to let Nati pass before shutting it and locking it behind them. The automatic motion sensor light flicked on in the hallway, sending the dark scattering.

"You always listen to me," Nati added, thinking of all the times Nati had come to Olivia looking for guidance, a sounding board or just a hangout buddy. Nati kept her angst far from her family, but Olivia was the exception, if only because she lived for gossip of every kind. Olivia was also remarkably insightful for someone who claimed to not be a big fan of human beings in general.

They made it up the stairs without incident. Once Olivia was sorted out in Val's former bedroom, Nati showered and put on her pajamas. Her head was clear by the time she hit the mattress. She kept going back to those years as a resident at the hospital alone, how hard she'd worked to make sure she fell asleep from sheer exhaustion. It had been a blessing after Leo left, her work providing the outlet she needed to drown out her grief over the end of their relationship. Leo had suggested a long-distance situation, but Nati had vetoed that idea right away. Being a resident was time consuming, stressful and not as well paid as being a practicing physician. Add to that the student loans she'd inevitably had to take out despite her family's support and Papi's hatred of debt, and there was no way she and Leo could have made it work. And she was not going to let Leo fund that situation, though he'd even offered to do so.

He'd fought her every step of the way. But when Zoraida had told her he was thinking of turning down the residency and finding something closer to Nati, that had sealed it for her. She refused to be responsible for his giving up any opportunities. She knew what it had cost them to get to that milestone, and she wasn't going to watch him throw it away. Out of the question.

She was determined that they go their separate ways, and damn her, it had worked. She'd made him leave. He'd even gotten married, if there were any doubts that her actions were correct.

And now he was back, and it was as if those six years had never happened.

She wished for the bliss of exhaustion, the precipitous sleep that obliterated the aching in her heart through the sheer oblivion of a body worn out to the extreme. As long as Leo could've been a long-lost possibility that she could relegate to the darkest corners of her memory, she could have pulled it off. She could have lived her life and pushed the regret deep under layers of time.

But he was here and in all her spaces. He'd moved on without her, and he would be returning to his wife and the life they'd built once his father's illness was resolved one way or another. It was a hopeless situation, as it seemed destined to always be between them. She shouldn't feel excitement at the thought of him or fantasize about another life where they were together. She knew how dangerous this line of thinking was. What's done is done, and there was no sense wishing otherwise.

Convincing her heart of this fact was another matter entirely.

Chapter Six

Leo

East Ward General Hospital was twice the size of Leo's hospital in California but lacked the picturesque polish of the university medical center, which had been built as much for style as for functionality. Where in California there were manicured lawns planted with soaring, pruned palm trees and jacaranda blooms that turned the walk-up to the emergency room into a canopy of purple every spring, there was only concrete and glass in this city, honking cars and racing pedestrians congesting the intersections. The noise level was so much higher in East Ward, though the traffic was somewhere north of surreal in LA, and the quality of the light was grayer here, powdered ink smudged over the streets and sidewalks.

The general gray scale of East Ward was broken up by fluffy white clouds racing across a bright blue sky that hung over the distant river, edges of sky limned in silver winking between buildings. It was such a contrast to the painfully pretty blue of a California sky over postcard-worthy landscapes. Leo couldn't help but admire the beauty of a Western valley, a desert or a slice of beach on the Pacific Ocean. But for all that, something in the gritty authenticity of East Ward spoke to him, made him feel welcome. Being back in the town of his childhood made him feel nuzzled and cocooned in familiar arms.

He arrived at the stout old building that housed the emergency department and thought of Nati for the hundredth time, wondering where she might be inside that building. If he weren't on leave, at this moment, he might be in surgery or doing consultations. He imagined what it would have been like to work alongside her. As a surgeon, he would have been called in to take on the critical patients she triaged. He would have even worked side by side with her on trauma cases that needed addressing directly in the ER on the days or nights their shifts overlapped. Not unlike the scenarios they'd always talked about when they were dating— Nati, who thrived on the dynamic and unpredictable nature of an emergency room, and Leo, who knew how to handle immense pressure with stoic solidity and relished the challenge of a finely wrought surgical procedure. When he worked, there were no insecurities or circular thoughts crushing his certainty. There was only whoever was in front of him, and it anchored him in a way few other things in life did.

A side door opened and two people in scrubs— probably nurses or technicians—stepped outside, lighting up their e-cigarettes for a quick vape. Leo felt a surge of longing for something to put in his hand and mouth but squelched the desire. He'd stopped smoking over a decade ago, and he wasn't going to tank his efforts. And anyway, his father was going home tomorrow. Things were already looking up.

He went inside, checking in with reception as usual, but instead of moving directly to the patient rooms, he took a detour with that air of belonging to a place that kept people from asking where he was going. He was familiar with the general layout of medical centers he'd worked at in the past, and now he used that knowledge and the posted signs to find his way to the emergency department, waiting for doors that required electronic cards to swing open for him to step inside. He scanned the nurses' station, belatedly realizing that there was no reason Nati would have the same shift every day or that she might have called in sick or switched schedules with someone, rendering all his efforts useless.

The person he couldn't stop thinking about burst into the space like a summer storm, examining a chart as she walked. He indulged the rare pleasure of watching Nati without being seen, his heart ripping a relentless beat in his chest.

Nati had her hair pulled back in a puffy bun, curls bounding out of the tie to frame her face. She looked like melted honey, all smooth and soft brown, the sheen of health emanating from her skin and hair and the shimmering gold of her eyes. She was everything that comforted him—cinnamon and cardamom, spiced wine and low-burning fires. She was more than beautiful, the look of her landing hard beneath his collarbone, and he had no choice but to put a hand over his chest, as if he could slow the throbbing of his blazing pulse.

She had told him once, in the afterglow of surrender, that he was her home, and he had believed her like the romantic fool he'd been. But even with all that had passed between them, his body reacted to her as if she'd never ended things with him—recognizing in her a soft place for his heart to land.

Perhaps sensing that she was being watched, she glanced up from her chart and looked him unerringly in the eye. She was at his side in a moment.

"Dr. Navarro," he said, calling up every last dredge of his strength to keep from melting directly into the floor.

"Dr. Espinoza," she said, glancing around her. He was grateful for the cover, even though he was hardly dressed as a medical professional. Her voice was as cool as the air that was pushing near-freezing temperatures through the hospital hallways. "Are you lost?"

"No," he said, attempting to match her cool tones. "I know exactly where I'm supposed to be."

Nati studied him, clutching the chart to her chest with white knuckles. Otherwise, her appearance was controlled and collected. Leo cast around for something—anything—to say. "ER keeping you busy?"

The slight cresting of an eyebrow was the only indication of her reaction. It was a step above talking about the weather, but it was all he had. "Always. Never worked an ER that didn't keep me busy."

True, because she had done her residency in the city and had obviously returned to East Ward once she'd passed her board examinations and become an attending physician. There were no dull hours in the ER of a metropolitan hospital.

Moments passed with excruciating slowness. He willed her to ask him something. Anything. He wanted to know everything about her, but perhaps he'd miscalculated. Maybe this was the confirmation he needed that she was not as interested in him. The chatty Nati he once knew had nothing to say to him.

"You do realize that it is a crime to trespass in secure medical areas," Nati continued, her voice stern with reprimand.

Or not.

"I am aware of this fact, yes. But I wanted to speak to you and couldn't risk waiting in my father's room and you deciding not to appear."

She tilted her head, her expression more like the mischievous cast he had once been so accustomed to seeing on her face, an expression that screamed *your audacity is getting the best of you.*

Handing the chart to one of the nurses, Nati said. "I'm taking my break. Page me if anything urgent comes through."

"Yes, Dr. Navarro," the nurse said.

"The cafeteria isn't far away," Nati said, waving at him to follow her. Pausing to greet a passing nurse, she said, "It must be weird being inside a hospital as a visitor and not on shift."

Leo relaxed. "It is. I feel powerless, despite the fact that my father has made many connections in the community over the course of his career here."

"He does get a lot of consideration as a result of who he is. But there is only so much you can do with your father's illness at the moment, except to explore your options."

"I hate this for him," Leo blurted out when they stopped in front of the elevator. Nati pushed the button. "He was always so tough and independent. I still can't believe that this is him."

Nati's face softened, the hard professional edge giving way to something that looked more like the Nati he once knew. "It must be hard for you to leave your wife and family behind to be here with your father. I'm sure he appreciates it."

Leo frowned at her words. "Didn't you… I'm not married anymore. Michelle and I finalized our divorce last year. We never got around to having kids, not with our work schedules. It was…easier to leave California than I thought, actually."

Nati's chewed her lip, her professional mask slipping while thoughts clearly raced behind those soft brown eyes. "You got married so soon after—" She truncated her sentence and turned away, walking quickly ahead and slipping inside a set of glass doors without glancing behind her.

Leo chest constricted. This was what he was looking for—an acknowledgment of what had happened, and hopefully an explanation from her for *why* it had happened. He desperately wanted her to finish her thought and nearly asked her to, but a group of residents crowded around them, making conversation difficult. When he was able to speak to her again, she held two cups of coffee in each hand, her expression neutral once more.

"Two creams, one sugar. Did I remember correctly?"

Such a small thing, but the fact that she had not forgotten released a flutter in Leo's chest. "Yeah. And you drink it—"

"However I find it," A smile sneaked in at the edge of her lips but she reined it in. "Something with your coffee?" Nati asked, indicating the muffins and packaged snacks close to the register.

Leo was feeling peckish but couldn't remember if he'd eaten breakfast. He picked up a chocolate chip muffin. "And you?"

"What's coffee without a side of sugar, right?" Nati scooped up a jelly-filled doughnut with a sheet of wax paper and placed it onto a small Styrofoam plate. Nati paid for their items before leading him to a table.

She stirred her coffee even though it was black, the doughnut sitting untouched. The tension was so thick, it choked him like the smoke from burnt oil, almost making his eyes burn.

"Nati, I…"

"Are your breaks as short as ours?" She looked up, then let her eyes slide away. "I guess I shouldn't complain. At least today I can sit down. Some days, I can barely grab a bite before I'm off again."

"It can be like that, sometimes," Leo said. "At home—" He paused, the word *home* tasting strange in his mouth. He was home now, but California had been home for six years. Now he was in a limbo between the two, unsure how to reconcile one with the other. "At my job, we try to schedule things out, but emergencies are the only constant in our work."

Nati nodded, giving him a small smile before taking a sip of her hot coffee, hissing from the heat. When she lifted her eyes to his, there was a plea in them, though he was out of practice at reading her unspoken signals.

"I wish we could talk, you know?" Leo charged ahead, only now understanding just how raw and exposed he felt since the moment he'd seen Nati in the waiting room of the ER.

Nati frowned. "About what?"

"Come on, Nati. You know about what."

Nati's eyes flashed large and bright, as if he'd caught her by surprise, before she schooled her features into something neutral again. God, she still did that, tried to look serious when things got emotionally charged. It was the opposite of her nature, even if he'd seen so little of that side of Nati since he'd returned. "This might not be the time or the place. My number is still the same. Or did you erase it from your phone?"

The ice in her voice was unexpected and sparked a surge of anger that took Leo by surprise. "My phone number is the same as well," Leo retorted. "If you had ever been interested, that would have been the best way to reach me."

Nati's eyes flashed again, this time with another emotion that burned away the thin veneer of her professionalism, revealing yet another side of her that he hadn't seen in too long. Another side that never failed to captivate him with its intensity. "You. Got. Married," she practically growled before jabbing her stirrer into the steaming black liquid.

"What is that supposed to mean, Nati? Am I supposed to feel guilty for moving on with my life after you decided you didn't love me anymore?"

Nati glanced around, no doubt to see if anyone had heard them, before setting her jaw, her face darkening with a flush that looked uncomfortable. "I'm not doing this." She stood suddenly, jamming her hands into her coat pockets before thinking better of it and scooping up her coffee cup. "I have to work now."

Nati turned and left the cafeteria without a backward glance. Leo sat, dumbfounded by the turn of their conversation. His anger had been sudden, fierce and surprising, a feeling he thought he'd moved past years ago. Even more surprising was the sharpness of Nati's anger in turn, which he could not understand. She'd left him. What was there for her to be angry about?

He toyed with his muffin, picking at it until it was nothing more than a pile of crumbs, going over their conversation, unable to pinpoint exactly where things had gone wrong. Only Nati could tell him where he'd misstepped, and he wasn't sure she would be so readily inclined to speak to him again.

Leo stepped out onto the pavement in front of the visitors' exit at the end of the day, feeling like he'd been repeatedly run over by the portable MRI machine. His mother and sister would stay with his father tonight. The sun was low—it would be dark by the time he made it home—but cast a golden-orange glow on the glass of buildings, reflected off mirrors and metal accents of cars parked along the curb. The burn in his stomach from his conversation with Nati had died down, leaving a generalized sense of exhaustion. His stomach rumbled and he wondered what he could pick up on the way home so he wouldn't have to cook tonight, when a familiar figure appeared at the employee exit. Leo recognized Caleb, decked out in jeans and a T-shirt that emphasized his muscles. Tahira stood a few paces behind, her hair wrapped in a gorgeous, shimmering green headscarf that complemented the warm geometric pattern of her dress. The glare she gave him, however, was as cold as an ice storm.

"Leo Espinoza," Caleb said, crossing his arms and looking Leo up and down. Leo wasn't sure he was ready for another confrontation, but this one was inevitable. "Finally back in East Ward."

"Caleb. Tahira." He burned with shame as he spoke. "It's good to see you both."

"Is it?" Tahira answered, every word and gesture dripping in defiance. "It has been forever—by no fault of our own, I might add." Tahira had always been one to come out swinging. At least that hadn't changed. A large truck rumbled by, drowning out every sound for a few moments until its overworked diesel engine faded into the distance.

"Yeah," Caleb added. "You just up and disappeared. That was a real crappy move."

"You're right. I wish I had been better. I wish…" The nostalgia he'd experienced all these years in California for the friends of his heart welled up in him. He'd made other friends whom he valued greatly, but none had been like Caleb and Tahira. "I'm sorry about that. After Nati, I just… I wasn't in a good place."

Caleb's face softened—he'd always been the most kindhearted out of the four, the first to make peace, the first to forgive. "I know your breakup with Nati was hard. I just wish you had let us be there for you. It's not like we didn't try."

They had tried. They'd called and sent messages. It was Leo who couldn't take the reminders of that life he'd had with Nati. Leo took Caleb by the shoulder and squeezed. "I paid for cutting you two off. I missed what we had so much. Can you forgive me for being a poor friend?"

Tahira's eyes grazed over him in distinct disapproval, her sharp nose almost made for looking down at him. But he took the impertinence in stride. If he wanted to get Tahira back, he'd have to let her come to him on her own time. She had never been one to be rushed.

"Are you going back to California?" Tahira asked.

Each time he asked himself this question, he came up blank—or worse, with a different answer each time.

"Yes. I believe so."

"Hmm…" Tahira continued. Caleb bit back a smirk. Leo knew this routine and allowed her the windup.

"You haven't changed too much," she continued, examining the entirety of him.

"Thanks," Leo said, his enthusiasm erupting but quickly cut off by Tahira's words.

"You haven't improved as much as I would have expected, either. Aren't you eating? Getting enough sleep? You might want to look into a multivitamin for that pale skin."

Caleb chortled from behind her, and even Leo couldn't keep the twitch from his lips. "You can say it, Tahira. I look like crap."

"Yes." A hint of a smile pulled at the edges of her lips but changed to a frown. "I'm sorry about your father."

Leo nodded, accepting this. "Probably why I look like crap."

Caleb clapped a hand on his shoulder in a clear gesture of sympathy. "You're allowed to, under the circumstances."

"Yes," Tahira said. "You get a pass. For now." Her words gave Leo hope that she might be softening toward him. But unless she'd changed completely, he knew she would make him work for it. Not like Caleb, who had been his friend before he'd had anything to do with Nati and had obviously already forgiven him.

Leo had been a fool. Instead of nurturing his connection with his friends, he'd let his breakup with Nati dictate too many things in his life. Standing in front of Caleb in all his sweet transparency, and Tahira, a tight, compact mass of fire and indignation on a good day, Leo felt the years of their separation ram into him like the impact of a train. He couldn't recuperate lost time, but maybe he could take steps to fix things with them.

"I'm staying with my sister down by the waterfront. Do you want to come over? I still remember how to make those drinks you both used to like so much."

Tahira stared at him for a moment, her dark brown eyes narrowing, concentrating fiercely on Leo. "It's been a long time. A long, long time."

"I know." He spread his hands. "I don't have a good reason for keeping to myself except that these last years were a little rough and, honestly—" Leo rubbed the back of his neck now, his nerves turning him into a collection of disparate tics in the body of one person "—the longer I went without communicating with you, the harder it became to…you know, communicate with you."

Caleb gave him a look that matched Tahira's, complete with knitted brow and narrowed eyes. He put his hands on his hips, shaking his head all the while until his face broke into a wide smile. "Man, if you ever pull that mess on us and disappear again…"

It was as if the sun had come out explicitly to shine on him, the warmth filling Leo's heart to overbrimming. This was his first victory since coming to East Ward, and he couldn't help but throw his arms around Caleb and lift him off his feet. Damn, he was heavier than he looked, probably the result of the testosterone he took to keep up his muscle mass. He set a laughing Caleb down and turned to Tahira.

"If you swing me around, I'm going to hit you with my bag," Tahira warned.

"Right." Leo pulled back, gratitude forcing tears from his eyes. He laughed them away. "I've just missed you both so much. You have no idea."

Caleb laughed in response, his eyes a little bright as well. "Prove it to me. Throw a little dinner in with that offer."

Leo's excitement peaked. "*De verdad*? We can stop off at the grocery store. You tell me what you want and I'll make it."

Tahira put her hands up. "I have to be at my mother-in-law's house, and if I am late, I will never hear the end of it."

"You mean there is someone in the world capable of intimidating you?" Leo asked.

"Oh, you have no idea," Caleb chimed in, to which Tahira gave him a look full of daggers.

"I'm intimidated by no one, but I prefer not to be nagged to the end of my life for the sake of family harmony."

Leo took both her hands in his. "It was good to see you again, my friend."

Tahira sniffed, but it felt more theatrical than real. "I expect a full dinner from you. You can't take back your promise."

Leo laughed. It felt good to be with them again. "I promise."

"Good." She tapped the side of his face before pulling herself together. "One last thing. Talk to Nati. Work that situation out, before you end up running off to California for another decade. Like Caleb said, we won't forgive you a second time."

Leo felt the joy drain out of him, remembering his earlier conversation with Nati. He shrugged. "We'll see. It hasn't been easy so far."

"There's a lot of history to work through," Tahira said. "I have faith in you both." She nearly jumped at the sound of a phone vibrating. Rummaging through her bag, she found the source of the noise and read the notification on the screen. "Ugh, the mother-in-law is messaging me again. I really must go." She gave them each a goodbye kiss before quickly walking toward the bus stop.

He and Caleb watched her departure until she disappeared around the corner. Caleb turned and draped an arm around Leo's shoulders, moving them away from the hospital. Leo didn't care where they went. This was Caleb. They'd been friends through every version of themselves since high school, and Leo felt an integral piece of himself slot into place.

"I'm hungry," Caleb said. "There's an Italian place up here that makes the best tortellini you've ever tasted. A lot of us stop in there after our shift to unwind. Let's hit that. You can make me a cocktail another time."

Leo responded by snaking his arm around Caleb's waist, giving him a quick squeeze that forced a yelp from him. "It's a deal."

They pulled apart, chatting about the hospital as they walked, dodging the steady pedestrian traffic. Caleb turned them onto a side street where a restaurant with an enormous Italian flag sat back from the sidewalk. The name *L'Abruzzese* was painted in green, white and red on an awning that covered an outdoor dining area. Leo smelled the tomato sauce and olive oil from where he stood, and the aroma tugged at his empty stomach.

"I feel like I haven't had a decent meal since Papá got sick."

Caleb paused at the steps of the restaurant, a hand on the ironwork of the awning. "I'm so sorry about that. I was there when the code team stabilized your dad, you know."

"I didn't." Leo pulled Caleb in for a hug. "Thank you."

Caleb patted his back, a soothing warmth between the tense valley of his deltoids. "That's how we do. I just hope he gets better."

So similar to Nati's response. It was part of the oath they'd sworn. To cure and care, and do the least harm. But that didn't mean Leo couldn't be grateful.

They made their way to the host station and were seated outside under the awning they'd walked by earlier. Leo could almost relax for the first time in days.

"You remember that clinic we used to always talk about?" Caleb said.

"The free clinic we dreamed of opening in East Ward? Sure I do. Why?"

Caleb paused to give the waitress their drink order.

Leo stopped her and asked for a prosecco—he felt like celebrating that he'd gotten two of his friends back.

"Nati, Tahira and I started it last year." He gave Leo a smile that beamed with pride.

"You did it? You opened a free clinic in East Ward?"

"Just a small operation right now. We do walk-ins, vaccinations, school physicals, some primary care, as well as free contraceptives and referrals to women's clinics in the area. We work with the state to service indigent patients, no ID or insurance required. That was a big win. We are also LGBTQ friendly—even got ourselves listed in the Rainbow Directory. But we still need things—a new ultrasound machine, some smaller diagnostic and testing equipment and more hours for our office manager so we aren't going in and taking turns doing paperwork."

Leo listened to Caleb as he described the clinic, the steps they'd taken to bring it into being, as well as the grant they were hoping they'd be awarded that would help them meet their goals. Leo was happy for his friends, but it was a hollow joy. Because of his actions, he hadn't been a part of their shared dream to open the clinic—or any of their other aspirations. He'd missed out on so much, and while he could blame Nati for breaking up with him, it was his decision to cut off the people who cared the most for him. He'd thought that by staying away from them, it would make it easier for him to get over Nati. But that had been a coward move. Letting his unresolved feelings for Nati rule his decisions only ruined relationships that, he realized, still meant so much to him.

"What other funding do you have?" Leo asked.

"State and federal funds, mostly. We also fundraise and pretty much beg for donations of every kind. We are currently preparing a presentation for the grant I mentioned. If it goes through, it will be a huge step forward for us." Caleb smiled at the waitress as she left their drinks and took their dinner order.

"I have some experience in grant writing," Leo said, swirling his glass of prosecco. "Want another set of eyes?"

Caleb grinned. "I'll have to check with Nati and Tahira, but I don't see why not."

"Tahira," Leo breathed. "She's scary. She was never a forgiving kind of woman."

"She'll be okay. She'll verbally destroy you for a while, but she'll get over it." Caleb sipped his prosecco and smacked his lips. "Man, this tastes good."

Leo shivered at the thought of Tahira meting out punishment like a goddess of old. He laughed as Caleb took another drag of prosecco, hissing as the bubbles tickled him. Leo was happy his selection had gone over well. "And let's not talk about Nati. We didn't exactly leave on the best of terms last time we spoke."

Caleb's face became shuttered. "That's because y'all have history. By the way, how's your wife?" Caleb said, and it sounded like a challenge. Leo couldn't help but respect his desire to protect Nati from harm.

"I'm divorced." Leo put his hand up so Caleb could examine the ring finger. "See? Not even a tan line."

"Hmm," Caleb said, still uncertain. "Okay, so you

came back to East Ward to take care of your dad. You have plans to get Nati back, too?"

Leo forgot how brutally honest they'd once been with each another. Sometimes it could be a lot, but it was usually what Leo needed to hear. "Nati doesn't want me. She broke up with me, remember?" Leo leaned back, rolling his head as if loosening his muscles might also unclog his brain.

"I wasn't asking about her. I was asking about you. Feelings?"

Leo took another long draught of his prosecco. "It would be a lie to say that there aren't feelings there. She was my first love, you know? That never goes away."

"For most people, it actually does go away. Especially when it was a traumatic breakup and you happened to get married right after," Caleb said.

"It wasn't right after," Leo protested.

"It was six months. A marriage that, I might add, you didn't even bother to invite us to."

Leo frowned. "I wasn't sure if you would want to go—not after everything with Nati."

"See, that's the problem with you. You keep filtering everything through your experience with Nati instead of treating your relationship with others as independent of her. Come on. We aren't symbionts. Tahira and I are your friends, too. Wish you had treated us that way."

Shame sent color flooding through Leo's cheeks. "Like you said, it was a traumatic breakup, you know?

At least for me. Not sure Nati experienced it the same way."

Caleb shook his head. "I'm not going to speak for Nati. That's not my place. But she changed after you guys broke up. I mean, our residencies were hard on all of us, but Nati took it to another level. She was *always* at work. You know how she is. She'll smile through an execution if she thinks she has no choice but to be tough. But she put herself through it. Not even Tahira put in the hours Nati did."

Leo shook his head, unable to believe that this critical part of her character had been influenced by their situation, especially given events of late. "I'm going to share this with you in confidence. Please don't tell her."

"I won't. I'm neutral, especially if you feed me."

Leo smiled at this. "I'm still a little pissed at how things ended."

Caleb gave him a sympathetic nod. "That's because you didn't want it to end. You didn't get that closure you needed."

"She's not why I'm here," Leo said. "I'm here for my family."

"Yeah, but it's also where the love of your life lives," Caleb chuckled, sipping his prosecco. "Might as well be efficient and work a little closure into your plans as well."

"Fair point." Leo waved their waitress over, indicating he wanted another glass.

"Still into those spirits, I see," Caleb laughed.

"You know I love good booze. That's never going to change. Alcohol and coffee keep me alive."

"Damn. Just like Nati," Caleb chuckled, and Leo felt the tease in his voice. Caleb's eyes flicked up to the door behind Leo, and his chuckle became a wide grin. "Speak of the devil."

Leo turned just in time to see Nati walk in with her brother, Rafi, and his husband, Étienne, who he recalled from the photos that Nati had showed him. "What are the chances?"

Caleb shrugged. "She's probably just getting off work."

"Does her sister know she's being unfaithful to the family restaurant?" Leo joked.

Caleb smiled at this. "They're closed, dummy. Remember?"

Leo's memory jogged into place. Navarro's was only open for breakfast and lunch. "A lot can change in six years."

Rafi saw him first. Even from where Leo was sitting, he could see the narrowing of his eyes and the pinched expression on his face. Rafi had always been friendly to Leo, but it made sense that, after the breakup, he'd feel overprotective of his sister. Nati, alerted by her brother's reaction, followed Rafi's stare and saw Leo. Before Leo could react, Caleb was waving a stone-faced Nati over to their table.

Leo recalled their awkward conversation in the elevator, how it had ended on an almost antagonistic note. He schooled his features, hoping not to get mired in a similar situation.

Chapter Seven

Nati

Nati had trouble forgetting about Leo and the bold nerve of him bringing up the past like that in her hospital. The endless bombshells that began when his father showed up in her ER showed no sign of abating. Nausea had broken over her when he'd told her he was divorced. Divorced! So quick to marry and…for what?

It was a waste, pure and simple, and no matter how many different ways she flipped the situation, it was clear as daylight that this, too, was her fault. She'd ended it with him—brutally and definitively. She couldn't speak to the quality of his marriage or what had happened during that time, but it was dawning on her that had she not sent him away, he might have been here, with her, *with her*, not off on the other side of the country, divorced and in pain and—she really needed to get a grip. This was not her. Nati Navarro was ruthlessly optimistic, tough as stone, ambitious to a fault and unapologetic. All these feelings that Leo was dredging up were rusty and unfamiliar from lack of use. Guilt, longing, nostalgia, regret, desire. She kept shoving them down, but they kept popping up again at the worst possible times. She hadn't wanted to break up with him. It had shredded her to pieces, driven her tendency to overwork, informed some of the more ill-advised affairs she'd had with men and women she'd stumbled on through her life. Just when she thought she'd come to terms with that loss, he'd shown up again to dig up every last memory that they shared, right to the bitter end.

Thank God for her brother and her brother-in-law, who wanted to talk babies all day, every day. She'd hoped that, when Rafi and Étienne met up with her after work for dinner, Leo would disappear from her thoughts and allow her head to be filled with beautiful brown babies topped with curly dark hair, enormous eyes like Étienne's and toothless smiles that would wreck her heart forever. An aspect of life she might not experience for herself, given her work and how busy it kept her, but she could live vicariously through them.

She was not prepared to have Caleb wave her over to a table the moment she arrived at the restaurant, Leo sitting right across from him like an apparition. The odds were clearly not in her favor lately. She looked away as quickly as she could before Leo caught her staring at him, but it was too late. His expression of surprise matched her own.

"Is that Dr. Sabroso?" Rafi asked, elbowing her in the side. "I didn't know he was back in town."

"Ugh, not with the nickname," Nati retorted before getting ahold of herself, forcing her face into a neutral expression. "It's a recent development." She didn't want to give Rafi any more ammunition to tease her. Just because he was married and planning a family didn't mean he was the paradigm of maturity.

"Your ex-boyfriend?" Étienne asked.

"Yeah, unfortunately." She bit the inside of her lip before coming to a decision. "I should go over and say hi. Meet you guys at the table?"

Rafi's visibly straightened, as if that was going to make him look ferocious. "Need us to go with you? We can be your backup."

Étienne put a hand on Rafi's shoulder. "Perhaps we will leave Nati to her business and you and I will see to ours. What do you think of that?"

"But…" Rafi protested, genuinely distressed that he would not be accompanying Nati to, who knows, make evil eyes at Leo or collect gems of embarrassing moments to tease her with later. Rafi was capable of anything.

"*But* nothing. We will order drinks and appetizers and leave Nati in peace. They have that artisan beer you enjoy so much," Étienne said, as if enticing a child away from the edge of a mud pit with the promise of a sparkling new toy. "Come. You know we are eating for two now."

Rafi gave him a disbelieving glare. "That's actually not how our version of baby-making works."

Étienne draped an arm over Rafi's shoulder, giving it a squeeze that effectively held him in place, and led him away from Nati. "I say sympathetic eating is very much how our version of baby-making works." He lowered his voice, but not low enough. "Among all the other enticing ways our babies are made."

They were so cute, it was nauseating. Étienne gave Nati a wink over Rafi's shoulder, which she answered with a grateful smile before he pulled a still-protesting Rafi, who managed to throw a last withering glare in Leo's direction, to the host stand. Teasing was the Navarro family's primary love language, and Nati would not have spared him had the situation been reversed. But overprotective Rafi, trying and failing at ferocity, was the last thing she needed. She wove through chairs and tables until she was at the far edge of the patio and in front of where Caleb and Leo sat.

"What a coincidence," she said with her signature singsong voice. Light and airy—it was her automatic default approach to everyone, no matter what emotional calamity she was undergoing. She dipped her head to offer Caleb an air kiss, hesitating a split second before offering her cheek to Leo as well. They were in public, after all, and she had been taught enough manners to behave properly.

That kiss, however, was a giant miscalculation. His familiar smell sent an arrow of heat and animal desire straight to her core, practically knocking her back. He smelled exactly as he had when they were together, right down to the cologne he wore, a brand she'd always gifted him because it complemented him and made him smell downright edible. After six years, she would not have expected him to continue using the same brand, but here he was, the aroma of his body spilling out from the worn pages of her memory, and it triggered every kiss, every touch he'd ever given her. It had her reeling on wobbly legs like she'd stepped off a carousel.

"Great minds…and stomachs…think alike," Caleb answered.

"Yes, they do," she said, searching for control of her breathing. Leo's scent had her by the throat and wouldn't let go. "Just, um, stopping by to wish you *buen provecho*," she finally forced out. Good manners also demanded that she keep her cool and not show how affected she was by Leo's presence, but she was failing at that as well.

Leo looked past her to where Rafi and Étienne were disappearing inside the door of the restaurant. "You're with Rafi?"

Nati glanced back at where she'd left Rafi but was not able to see him or Étienne any longer. "Yes, and Étienne. They're expecting their first child by the end of the year…" Nati's voice trailed off as she realized her nerves were causing her to overshare. Rafi and Étienne had met at her graduation party, which took place within a few short months of her breakup with Leo, and she had tied those two events inextricably in her brain.

"A child? I'm genuinely happy for them." Leo had

met Nati's family back when everyone was still single, long before Val got together with Philip. Leo had been the only boyfriend Nati had introduced to her family, which had made their breakup all the more difficult for its effect on the Navarros, who had grown to accept him as one of their own.

"The years get away from you," Caleb interjected, carefully studying Nati and Leo. She'd get an earful from Caleb later on, of that she was almost certain. "Especially when you go MIA—just saying."

"You're never going to let me forget that, are you?" Leo muttered.

"Hell, no, I won't. Oh, and did you know, Val's married, too?" Caleb added.

"He knows, Caleb." Nati really wish she could kick him in the leg and get him to cut her loose so she could get back to Rafi and Étienne.

"She got married the year before Rafi did. Étienne was the best man. Isn't that how Rafi and Étienne finally got together, Nati?"

"Yeah, something like that," Nati muttered. Caleb could be quiet anytime now.

Leo shook his head in disbelief. "I guess that just leaves you, right?"

Nati felt those words land like a series of punches across her body. She clamped down on her reactions, willing her face to go blank. Keeping her emotions in check and projecting good humor was always the safest choice. Caleb shifted in his chair, looking everywhere else but at her. Nati had never been one to dream of marriage or children. She was all about her career and doing as much good as possible in the world. But the topic had come up between her and Leo, and he had been the only person she could have ever imagined such a thing with. Now that it had long since ceased to be a possibility, the reminder stung.

She unhooked her clenched jaw. "Well, I don't want to leave Rafi and Étienne waiting."

"If you guys want to join us…" Caleb said, but the invitation was delivered as if he already knew what the answer was going to be.

"It's fine." A waitress slipped by, setting down steaming plates of tortellini in cream sauce topped with sage leaves before them. "We haven't even ordered yet, and you are getting ready to eat." Nati indicated with a chin nod toward their dishes. "You'd better start before your dinner gets cold."

"Nothing worse than eating cold food," Leo said, watching Nati with an intensity that very nearly stole all her words from her. It was an admonishment Nati had used many times when they'd been together, something she had absorbed from her family—hot foods should be hot, cold foods should be cold. There was nothing worse than eating a tepid meal.

He'd remembered that. She didn't allow herself to read too much into it.

"Well, good night," Nati said, waving to them both.

"*Cuidate*, Nati," Leo said. Nati turned briefly, held his gaze.

Cuidate, Nati, ya que no puedo. Take care of yourself, since I can't anymore. The last thing he'd said before she'd sent him away while she drowned in the lack of him without anything to keep her afloat. The look in his eyes told her he knew exactly what he was saying, though he was playing innocent in front of Caleb. She smiled—no, she *beamed*—pretending that she hadn't caught the innuendo. She had long relegated him and everything that had to do with him to the past, but he simply refused to stay there.

Nati turned, clutching her purse close to her as she made her way inside the now-busy restaurant, searching for Rafi and Étienne. They were sitting, heads close together, as if they were sharing secrets meant only for each other. Their affection, subdued and discreet in public, was obvious to anyone who had eyes to look—the subtle angling of their bodies toward each other, their eyes that held each other's gazes far longer than necessary, Étienne's long arm draped around the back of Rafi's chair. She felt their connection like a palpable thing between them.

Being with a couple so obviously in love, especially if one of them was her brother, wasn't usually a trial for Nati. Romance simply didn't make up the bulk of her thinking when there was so much else to do.

Now, the sight of them made her chest ache and ache. She'd had this, too. Once upon a time. And hadn't been able to find it again.

She slid into her chair, tucking her purse onto her lap. "Sorry. Caleb was feeling chatty."

Rafi unstuck his attention from Étienne, which Nati instantly regretted. "You mean Dr. Sabroso was chatty," he said, waggling his eyebrows.

Nati rolled her eyes at her brother. "Not in the mood."

"Sorry, but being in the mood is not a prerequisite for being teased," Rafi retorted. "We die like heroes."

"I'm not a hero and neither are you, so zip it," Nati snapped before gathering her wits about her. It wasn't Rafi's fault that Leo had left her so undone. "What did you order?"

"More hors d'oeuvres than would be healthy for any of us to eat," Étienne answered.

Rafi gave him his most wounded expression. "I'll remind you that you ordered the sampler. Don't throw me under the bus."

"One sampler. Not three."

"They're tiny. Nati will inhale them all before we even have a chance to try them."

Nati quirked her lips into a half smile. Rafi and Étienne gave good banter and it was just the right amount of levity that she needed. "He's not wrong there. I worked twelve hours and all I had was a boiled egg."

Rafi chortled. "Don't tell me dad pawned off his boiled eggs on you, too."

"He did!" Nati said, a small giggle erupting from her despite her sour mood. Leave it to her family to be so unintentionally ridiculous that they almost made her forget her preoccupations. Almost. "Why is he making so many boiled eggs?"

Rafi spread his hands, one landing on Étienne's thigh, which he squeezed. "He said he was making potato salad and cooked too many. All I know is he better not eat them all. His doctor warned him about his cholesterol."

"And his blood pressure. If he doesn't behave, he's going to end up with a serious health problem on his hands," Nati said.

"That's what happened to my father," Étienne interjected. "Too much stress, eating on the run and not enough exercise, which, over time, contributed to his stroke. It took him almost two years to recover adequately."

"He walks every day, but I wish Papi would do more to avoid that outcome," Nati answered, taking a sip of water, relishing the sharp tang of the lemon slices she'd added.

"So Enrique is responsible for your love of drama *and* your collective stubbornness. Good to know," Étienne said fondly.

"You're one to talk," Rafi retorted.

Nati only half listened as they bickered playfully. Papi could retire anytime if he wanted to. Rafi and Val were both married. Nati had a full career that paid well and left her next to no time to help in the restaurant. Val was about to open a second restaurant of her own in the trendy waterfront area where she lived, and she had done everything possible, from training the staff of the original Navarro's restaurant to consolidating the management of the business ends of both so Papi wouldn't have to work as hard to keep up. The mortgage on the building that housed Navarro's practically paid for itself. There was no reason for Papi to wake up at four o'clock in the morning every day at his age and work as if he were still in his twenties. He did it because he wanted to, and it was taking its toll on his health.

Their server brought out their appetizers and took Nati's order—sautéed scallops with lemon over a bed of angel-hair pasta, and a spinach agrodolce. With her running around, she hadn't had a free moment to stop into the bathroom to wash her hands. It was an ingrained habit, since she couldn't go thirty minutes without washing and moisturizing her dry hands at work. She excused herself to find the restroom, purposely not glancing in the direction of the patio where Leo and Caleb were seated outside. She needed a minute to clear Leo out of her mind so she could focus on the arrangements for her future niece or nephew, who would be arriving in the world in about six months. She didn't want to weigh down what should have been an exciting dinner with echoes of a lost past. She needed to get out of her own head.

When she was done washing her hands, she opened the bathroom door and nearly ran into a broad chest and a familiar, arresting aroma.

"Leo," she gasped, all the air rushing out of her, replaced by the scent of his body.

"Nati," he said, and, by the way he stood, leaning casually against the wall, it was clear the only one surprised by this run-in was Nati. What was it with the universe always putting this man in her path?

"Sorry," he said, straightening. "Listen, I don't want to take you away from dinner with your family."

She wanted to stamp her foot in frustration. How could he be such a consistent, strategic pain in the ass? She breathed, sucking in more of the delicious smell of his body, and chose manners yet again. "We've only just ordered."

"Oh, good." He suddenly looked uncertain. "I think we got off on the wrong foot."

Nati frowned. "We didn't get off on the wrong or right foot." She thought about deflecting any further conversation on the matter, but there was relief in coming clean, putting everything out in the open. She waved a hand between them. "We have baggage, and it's making everything strange between us."

Leo dropped his eyes in a gesture of shyness she did not want to find adorable. "You're right. Things have been strange between us because of our…history. I just wish we could have a good talk. Get past all that." Leo nodded. "It would give me—us—the kind of closure we need."

Nati tilted her head to look up at him. She might as well have *confusion* written in bold letters across her face. "We broke up six years ago. You got married within six months. It seems to me like you found your closure, didn't you?"

Leo's expression softened, and Nati had to repress a powerful, familiar desire to run her hands through his hair, to soothe him and make everything better.

"And I'm divorced now. I was messed up after our breakup, and I made some decisions I shouldn't have. I…" Leo paused, breathing deeply as if to steady himself. "I still haven't stopped feeling the aftereffects. Maybe if I talk it out…"

Nati vibrated with tension. "Leo, what are you saying?"

Leo sighed, obviously struggling to find the words. "I know you're doing okay and I know you've moved on with your life—"

"Moved on," Nati murmured, her voice heavy with disbelief. He really hadn't figured out why she'd broken up with him. But she had made a hard decision and she couldn't allow herself to regret it.

And still, some stupid, childish desire at the back of her mind had wished that he'd fought his way back to her, even after everything. But why would he, when she hadn't fought, either?

Then he'd gotten married. As if she were just a cog removed from a space that he could fill with any other.

"I… I need this," he said quietly. "With everything happening with Papá, I'm not sure if I'm going back to California, or, if I do, when I'll come back again. This is the time to fix things, to make everything right, before the chance disappears."

What she heard in his voice wove its way deep inside her, landing in the wound that her heart had not been able to heal from, had barely been able to scar over. They were both looking for the same thing in the end, and maybe this was how they could cure each other.

"Now might not be the best time to have that conversation," she said finally.

Leo let out a shaky laugh at this. "No. But maybe we could get together, away from our families and the hospital and just…talk. That's all I want." Leo reached out, only brushing the very tips of his fingers along the edge of the white T-shirt that had come untucked from her jeans. But she felt the touch like a knife slicing through her tendons and bones. "Please."

Nati thought about what she needed, how it wouldn't be such a bad idea to wipe away the last remnants of that bitter past and try to move forward. Nati's entire family was moving headlong into the future. It was her turn to move on as well. She couldn't keep treating Leo the same way as when they were together. Six years and a lifetime of experiences had passed. It was time to grapple with who they were now and clear those dusty cobwebs out of their lives.

"What are you hoping for in the end, Leo?"

"We have history, I know, but maybe we can figure out a way to be friends."

Nati felt suddenly tired. *Friends*, she wanted to say. *Is that what we'll be?* The word was offensive, like a bruise coming out of nowhere. But what could she expect, after everything? This was already more than she thought she'd ever get, so much so that she hadn't even thought to simply ask for it. Because it was clear to her, after her emotional outburst of today, that she was still stuck in the mess she'd created and hadn't moved on very well, either.

"I know I said some…stupid things earlier. But here." She pulled out her cell phone, forcing him to scramble to pull out his. She surely had his number buried somewhere in her contacts, and most likely he still had hers, but this was just easier. It felt like starting fresh. Leo looked at her, tender and hesitant, and Nati nearly obeyed yet another old impulse to wrap her arms around him, nullify their mutual discomfort with the familiar press of her body against his and sink into the promise that his touch had always delivered. It had always been hot between them, like gas meeting a flame, and they could often get away with saying very little but communicating so much through their eyes, their hands, their skin. But many times, it had also been like this—vulnerable and soft and full of a fundamental belief that each would serve as a barrier for the other against the pain of the outside world.

Except Nati had brought that pain inside their walls. No matter how she rationalized it, this was on her. Even if she had been compelled by things more powerful than her—the culmination of years of study, the promise of dreams realized, the satisfaction of a well-earned career. But what had been the cost?

And what was stopping them now, except for time, fear, and the strangeness of knowing a person so deeply and yet discovering that there were things that were no longer recognizable in them?

They exchanged numbers. When Nati tucked her phone away, she said, "I should… I need to get back to Rafi and Étienne before they get worried."

Leo started, as if he'd been pulled from his own journey within a memory. "Of course. Good night, Nati." He stepped aside, making his bulk smaller to allow Nati to pass. "And thank you for…for this."

She nodded, not trusting herself to speak, and squeezed by him, ignoring the heat of his body that pulled every tiny hair on her skin straight and taut as if magnetized. The very proximity of him rippled down her skin and slammed her heart around in her chest.

She hurried back to her table, where Rafi and Étienne sat engrossed in each other. At least they'd left her some appetizers.

She pulled herself together. She only had to pretend for a few more hours before she could go home and allow herself to process the events of what had turned into yet another impossibly long day.

Chapter Eight

Leo

Leo returned from dinner that evening feeling lighter than he had in months, possibly years. The end of his relationship with Nati was an outstanding wound that had had far-reaching repercussions in his life. The hope of finding a way to navigate that situation, of finding an equilibrium that would allow him to close this chapter in his life and move on, was one he could not relinquish. This was their chance to make things right and put to rest those feelings once and for all. He hated the way things had ended between them and the way they behaved with each other now, as if they were an unknown quantity to be avoided at all costs. Or worse, to treat each other like strangers who had never shared anything of importance, one person like any other on the streets. When he left East Ward now, he would have tied all his lose ends, left no unresolved issues. He would be ready to meet the future.

He was aware that he'd cornered Nati and hated that for her, but she was slippery and would have continued to evade him even though there was so much that needed be said. He wanted the life he was trying to build to be different from what he'd had before, and making peace with Nati was an integral part of that. If he had let her get away tonight, he knew he would have lost his chance to make things different between them.

His father finally left the hospital a few days after his conversation with Nati to his mother's home, where the family would coordinate care. There were chemotherapy appointments Leo would need to keep, and visits to specialists proposing different treatments for the cancer that was eating away at him. But Papá seemed to flourish in the company of his children and his ex-wife. More and more, Leo was glad that he'd returned.

His phone dinged in his mother's kitchen, where he was balancing a cup of coffee, a croissant and a bowl of fruit. He set everything down on the counter and looked at his notifications. To his surprise, the message was from Nati. He opened it without hesitation.

Caleb mentioned you wanted to look at the grant proposal.

Leo typed quickly. I did. The offer still stands.
Three dots appeared, then, Want a tour of the clinic?

Leo was stunned. He blinked quickly, making sure that he wasn't dreaming her text before answering Hell yeah!

The laughing emoji that came next loosened something in his chest. She followed with I have tomorrow off. I can show you the clinic and run through the proposal and presentation, if that works for you.

I'll check with Genevieve and give you a confirmation.

Nati's thumbs-up emoji came through, and he fired off a quick message to his sister about possibly staying with their father the next day. Genevieve responded quickly.

I can do it. What's your important appointment?

Leo shook his head as if his sister were right in front of him. Nosy.

Curious, that's all.

Leo fired off a Stay curious before messaging Nati.

I'm free tomorrow.

It was a full ten minutes before Nati's response came through. Sorry so slow. Still at work. Tomorrow, 10 a.m. Sending address now.

The address of the clinic came in on the next text. It was in a neighborhood Leo barely recognized, even after pulling it up on his GPS. Before he got too caught up in trying to situate the clinic, he sent a return message, thanking Nati and confirming he'd be there at the time she'd designated. Leo wanted to punch the air. He was happy—about being of use, about the clinic and about the prospect of spending the day with Nati.

Leo brought his father soup for lunch and set the tray on the end table in his bedroom. Papá was reclining against the enormous pillows of his bed, drowsing peacefully to the sound of El Gran Combo coming through a very expensive set of wireless speakers he'd purchased for himself earlier in the month. Leo's father had told him when it arrived that this would most likely be the last illness he would have to endure in his life, and he wanted very much to at least enjoy the sound of impeccable music while he could. Leo couldn't fault his father for this.

"When is the last time you heard them play live?" Leo asked.

Papá opened his eyes, the same brown-green as Leo's. In fact, Leo had gotten a lot from his father— his green eyes, the auburn-tinted hair, the shape of his face. Only his skin was paler than Leo's, which was as an olive-tan much like his mother's.

Papá adjusted himself in the bed among his cascade of pillows in preparation for his lunch. He was still weak from his cardiac scare of the week before, but he was slowly returning to himself. "About three years ago. They are on tour again but I do not trust myself to attend a live concert anymore." Papá used his remote control to further lower the sound. "If I close my eyes and put the music up just right, these speakers make me feel like I am there."

"Worth the expense?" Papá had never been one to say no to his pleasures, but he was the kind to give himself a hard time when he spent the money, a reminder that he hadn't always possessed the means. But the guilt of spending so much money didn't bother him as much as he claimed.

His father observed Leo as he prepared the bowl on a freestanding dining tray. "You look like you are in a happy mood, *mijo*."

"Happy might be too strong of a sentiment, given the circumstances. But I do feel optimistic. Your doctor seems positive about the outcome of your next round of treatment. You just have to get better."

Papá nodded. "It's a better prognosis than I expected."

Leo nodded, adjusting his father's pillows. "You have to take every victory you can."

"That sounds like a good life lesson. How is Nati? I miss seeing her check in on me. Such a wonderful woman."

Leo held a spoonful of soup in shaky hands, having a quick taste to make sure it had not gone cold. "She's okay. She opened a free clinic. I'm going to meet her tomorrow so she can show it to me."

His father's face creased into a smile. "Are you going to make up with her? I always hoped you would get back together."

"Papá!" Leo said, handing his father the spoon. "I'm going to stop by and take a look at the clinic."

"Anything else?" his father probed, stirring his soup without looking at it. Leo really did not want to clean up a soup spill.

"Eyes on your bowl," Leo admonished before continuing. "I'm going to review her grant proposal. It would help the clinic if they were awarded that money."

His father took a sip of the hot liquid, savoring the flavors before he pressed Leo further. "And?"

"And what? Papá." Leo couldn't hold back his laughter. "Nothing else. It's not a date or anything. It's just two people collaborating to find a solution to a problem. I'm astonished by the way your brain works."

Papá sighed. "You can't blame an old man for hoping." He tapped his lips with a napkin. "I always did like Nati. She has fire. And she knows what it means to work hard. That's a woman standing on her own two feet, right there. Not flying in the clouds like too many others."

"She can't stand any other way," Leo retorted.

Papá gave him a withering look. "You do the right thing and get that girl back, *me oyes*? Listen to your old man."

"Okay, okay," Leo laughed, observing his father. He had color in his cheeks, his hair brushed and set with pomade, like most of the men of his generation. And while he was occupied with eating, he smiled easily and his eyes were bright. Leo had missed his father's spunk and mischievousness. Papá's illness might be stressful, but Leo loved being here with him.

"Don't let him overdo it," came his mother's voice from the open door of the room.

Papá's face brightened, and his mother, who could be dour and severe on the best of days, answered with a soft smile of her own.

"Leo is being a good boy. He made me soup and he's keeping me company."

"If you say so," she said, fondness in every word. Leo was never going to understand how two people who so clearly cared for one another had ever gotten divorced.

Mamá approached the bed, glancing inside of the soup bowl and flicking her eyebrows up as if to admonish Papá wordlessly to not leave anything behind. Papá simply chuckled at the expression and obediently took another spoonful.

"At least you are not too tired to give bad advice, eh?" Mamá said.

Papá set down the empty bowl, frowning. "What bad advice? I always give the best advice."

Here we go. Leo already knew what her complaint was and braced himself for it.

"Don't encourage him to make up with Nati." She took a seat at the edge of the mattress on the other side of his father. "Your son's life is so much better without her. He has an important position in one of the best medical centers in the country. He lives in a wonderful place, has many good friends from what I remember. Why would he throw all that away to come back here?"

"Who said he would throw anything away? Maybe he will bring her back to California with him," Papá retorted. In his excitement, he coughed loudly, prompting Leo to lean forward and pat his back.

His mother eyes narrowed to slits. "Is this true? Have you been giving this some thought, no matter how many times I warn you?"

"No, Mamá, but it's astounding the number of assumptions you make about Nati and me. And anyway, it's my business, right?"

"You are a grown man but it's my job to guide you. She's not good for you, that's all." Mamá reached over to grab the empty bowl of soup. "I'm going to put this in the kitchen."

Leo watched the way his mother snatched up Papá's empty bowl and hurried out of the room. He exchanged a glance with his father before getting to his feet.

"I've got to get to the bottom of this," Leo said.

"*Vete*. And good luck, because your mother is one of the most intractable people I have ever known."

Leo nodded before leaving the bedroom, debating on whether to close the door, opting to do so to allow his father to get more rest.

His mother was washing the bowl when he took the stool on the other side of the kitchen island. "What's going on? You haven't given Nati a break once since Papá got sick."

Mamá set the bowl carefully in the dish rack before meticulously wiping the down the sink. "I see the way you look at her."

Leo shook his head. "And how do I look at her?"

Mamá looked up from her work, letting the towel she was holding slip onto the counter, not spread out to dry as she usually did. His mother was fastidious about everything she did. "Like she's a meal and you haven't eaten in a long time."

"That's...quite a comparison."

Mamá's laugh was short and dry. "You're my son. I know you better than anyone, and I know you aren't over her yet."

Leo scrubbed his face. He could protest, but what was the point? His mom could see right through him. "I've never understood why you dislike her so much."

Mamá jabbed a finger at him. "Because she's too ambitious. You will never matter more than her getting ahead in this world. You need someone who will put you first."

Leo felt the fundamental wrongness of his mother's words, even as he lined them up with his experience with Nati and saw the overlaps. Nati's single-minded desire for success, her drive to be the very best. How easy it had been to let him go when their professional goals no longer aligned.

"You're wrong about Nati," he said, but his words sounded hollow even to his ears. Had her actions really proven otherwise? "But even if you were, that's not what's between us anymore. Nati is in the past, so there's no reason to keep bringing her up."

"I hope so." She leaned forward, hands planted on the counter. Even though Leo was bigger and bulkier than she was, his mother still managed to crowd him, make him feel like he was a kid all over again. "Because you will never find a position here like the one you have in California. Don't throw it away."

"A position? Or a life? What matters more, Mamá?"

Eyes flashing, she turned abruptly, stalking out of the room, leaving him alone with his words. He didn't want Nati back. He wanted peace, a sense of tying up that part of his life. He wanted to let that part of his past go so he could return to California and start a new chapter of his life. Not because of his job, but because he wanted to thrive in every way. His mother kept missing the mark.

But at that moment, California might as well have been on the other side of the solar system.

Leo was a wreck as he prepared to meet Nati at the clinic. He'd spent more time than he should have getting ready, as if it was his job. He had to constantly remind himself that he wasn't a volunteer physician on the clinic's staff. He wasn't even part of the committee evaluating the grant application. He was a surgeon on leave, present only in the capacity of knowledgeable professional, lending his expertise. He might even be counted as a friend in any other context. He didn't need to feel so nervous, and yet his hands shook when he tried to button up his dress shirt, and he dropped the belt he was looping through his slacks—possibly the first time he'd dressed up since he'd arrived in East Ward. It had taken only two weeks of his father's illness, Nati's appearance, and his mother's words to discombobulate him and make him forget all the habits and certainties he'd brought with him from California.

Leo tried to get his head in the game as he approached the building that housed the clinic. It was a good location. The low-to-mid-income neighborhood would benefit from the easy access to the medical services offered. From the outside, the structure looked spacious and well cared for. It was the type of real estate he had actually envisioned when they used to talk about their shared project. Of all the goals Leo had dreamed of achieving with Nati, this had been one of the most important ones.

And she'd achieved it without him.

Leo shoved the nostalgia and regret aside. He needed to be here, in the present. There was still so much that he could accomplish right now.

He walked through the door and found an older woman answering the phone behind the glassed-in reception area, voice heavy with a Caribbean Spanish accent. Three people, including a mother with a small child, sat in the guest area. The spaces were immaculate and welcoming with lots of wood, reading materials and soft seats that made waiting for an appointment as homey as possible. There was even a small Keurig station with a generous variety of coffees, teas and hot cocoas.

The door next to the front desk opened and out stepped Nati, dressed in an unbuttoned smock, pretty and fresh as a sunflower. Beneath her jacket, she wore a yellow dress that flared at the hips and ended mid-calf. A white cardigan with two buttons undone covered the top, in deference perhaps to the cold of the air conditioned room, a contrast to the spring warmth of the city outside. And her Crocs, of course, because Nati had always been fastidious about taking care of her feet and legs, given the demands of their profession. A tremor at the center of his being shook to life, a quake that had begun as admiration and was spiraling into the familiar anxiety of wanting and needing. In another life, he would have put his hands around the smooth slope of her waist and pulled her in for a good-morning kiss, his body already primed for that forbidden connection.

He balled his hands into fists instead. He was doing a favor for an old friend. That was all. He could handle this.

"Dr. Espinoza. It's so good to see you again. Come inside," she said with a too-cheery inflection that he understood was for the benefit of the handful of patients in the waiting area who would not take kindly to anyone skipping ahead of their turn to be seen. When she closed the door behind them, he found himself in the receptionist's office where Nati waited patiently for the tiny woman talking on the phone to finish her call and set the receiver in its cradle.

"Elena, this is Dr. Espinoza. He's going to be visiting with us today."

"Another volunteer!" Elena exclaimed, rising to her diminutive height, smiling brightly in her oversized scrubs. "It's so nice to meet you, Dr. Espinoza. Dr. Navarro will take very good care of you."

Leo smiled at the woman, her dark curly hair bouncing with enthusiasm around her shoulders. She seemed like an uncomplicated ray of sunshine, and Leo instantly liked her. "Thank you. I know she will."

Nati pinched her lip, clearly biting back a smile.

"Did you run that errand for me this morning?" she asked Elena.

Elena looked at Nati with almost maternal fondness. Leo fully expected her to reach out and squeeze Nati's cheeks at any moment. "Yes, I did! I put those doughnuts and coffee you asked for in your office, Dr. Navarro." She beamed again. "If you need anything at all, you just let me know."

"Thank you, Elena," Nati smiled and led Leo back to a small office he supposed was hers.

When they closed the door behind them, he said, "She seems like a happy person."

Nati gave a hearty laugh that transformed her into someone younger and more luminous. It was the laugh he recognized as her own, and his heart moved at the thought that she might be thawing toward him, becoming less guarded and more herself. She pointed to an empty chair in front of a consultation desk, which he sank into.

"She is. Jobs are hard to come by in this neighborhood ever since so many companies moved. Everyone has to commute into upper East Ward or other parts of the city to work. She has an autistic sister that she cares for, and this job is within walking distance from her house, so she goes above and beyond."

"She's committed to doing her part."

"She really is, and she's good at it, too. Everyone loves Elena." Nati walked over to the side credenza, where she picked up two lidded coffees, handing one to Leo. "Two creams, one sugar."

"Yeah. And you drink it—"

"—however I find it," they said in unison, dissolving into laughter. Nati's need for caffeine was so great, she had been known in college to eat coffee grounds if she had to.

"I am remarkably and nauseatingly consistent." She set down her cup and picked up the small box of doughnuts that were sitting next to the cups. "Sour cream doughnuts, right? You can't get the full effect of coffee without a plate of sugar to go with it."

"Where's your jelly-filled?" Leo retorted, picking up the doughnut with a napkin to keep his hands from getting too sticky. "Or are you finally watching your sugar intake?"

"Sugar is my friend. You can't part us." Nati smiled, bits of powdered doughnut covering the desk despite her efforts to be neat. Some of the fine white powder dusted her knuckles, and Leo had to physically push down an instinct to take her hand and lick the sugar clean.

He took a bite of his doughnut without tasting it.

"So," Nati said between mouthfuls, "I thought I'd show you the clinic and then we could go through and look at the grant packet. That way, the proposal will make sense."

"Sounds good." He paused, taking a sip of his coffee in an effort to steady himself. Being this close to Nati was wrecking his central nervous system. "I'm really glad you are letting me be a part of this, no matter how small."

Nati folded her hands, her face full of understanding. "We came up with so many of the ideas in school.

We were actually prescient of the needs of our current patients."

Leo nodded. "Poverty is universal and is usually addressed with similar strategies, no matter where it occurs."

Nati's grin was mischievous, and Leo wanted to fall into it. "I knew you'd say that." She leaned forward, dropping her voice. "You were right the other night. It's good for us to talk things out, try to come to some kind of resolution." She swept her hand out around her. "This was as much your dream as ours, and I love the idea that you might keep track of what we're doing here." Her expression dimmed, and suddenly, she was leaning back in her chair. "Even if you do plan on going back to California eventually."

Leo's stomach twisted at those words. He could feel in his bones the distance of every single mile between East Ward and California, as if he'd inhabited that place in a dream that belonged to someone else.

He had to pull himself together.

"I like that. Thank you." He paused, then added. "Plus, it would make Tahira happy, and we really try to keep Tahira happy."

Nati barked out a laugh at this. "Yes, we do. Tahira is not one to be trifled with."

Scooping up a clipboard, Nati tapped her lip, as if she hadn't mapped out this entire encounter, from the greeting to the moment he stepped outside the door to go home. He knew her too well to assume she'd left any of this visit to chance. "Well, then. First things first. I'm going to bore you to tears. We're going to go through the business end—scheduling, billing and record keeping. Just a brief overview to give you a context for our financial need based on patient demand. Then we'll conduct a few visits, with our patients' permission, of course."

"Of course." Leo chuckled.

He caught a glimpse of her clipboard and saw that he was right. She'd mapped out the entire morning, right down to quarter-hour intervals. "Dispensary, diagnostic, referral services… You're simulating a committee visit, aren't you?"

A sly smile spread across Nati's face. "Yes? I mean, you're as close as I'm going to get to a dry run with a medical professional who knows nothing about our facility."

"Okay, okay," Leo said between chuckles. "I see where this is going. Lunch had better be included in this little sales pitch."

"A working lunch." Nati tilted up her head, smiling sweetly, and all he wanted to do was lean down and meet her lips halfway. The taste of Nati would be sweeter than the doughnut he'd eaten.

"Ask me if it's busy."

The question was odd, but Leo decided to just roll with it. "Is it busy at your tiny neighborhood clinic, Dr. Navarro?"

Nati plastered a bland smile on her face, which was actually funnier than her stab at false sweetness. "It's always busy here, Dr. Espinoza. Our community assessment has demonstrated a demand for free and income-based care, and community demands are what drive our services. You'll also meet a few of our volunteer and permanent staff members. Everything regarding our back-office operations has been forwarded to your committee, but if you require clarifications, we can discuss them during debriefing. Any questions?"

"As usual, you've thought of everything."

"Of course. Were there ever any doubts?"

Leo knew her too well to have expected anything less. "None at all, Dr. Navarro. Lead the way."

They returned to the small business office at midday, where Elena had set up a selection of salads, sandwiches and fruit, perhaps more than Nati and Leo would eat. But knowing Nati, she'd give it all to Elena anyway. At least, that's what the Nati of once upon a time would have done.

They were still discussing the proposal she'd walked him through as they ate, including the general visit with a young patient with a persistent fever and rash whose parents did not have health insurance. It was the perfect example of their demographic—young families working multiple jobs, all of which offered few health care benefits. Nati settled in the worn leather office chair at the desk, inviting Leo to sit across from her. "We routinely study these processes to cut out redundancy and waste while still remaining compliant precisely because we don't have the workforce to manage the flow of documentation. We'd rather use those funds to interact directly with patients."

"That's actually a good approach. Show with concrete data that whatever funds you're awarded will go directly to enhance patient care and not to overhead or administrative costs. Emphasize the total number of face-to-face hours patients spend with a physician versus administrative expenditures—it's to your advantage that Elena is currently not a full-time employee. Show them you are as streamlined and efficient as you can be. I think that's one of the things that makes this clinic so strong—you're trying to do a lot with very little, and you're succeeding."

Nati dipped her head in acknowledgment. "I do most of the begging for the clinic, and there are community initiatives, but as large and varied as this community is, East Ward is not a rich enclave. We have to work with what we have."

"I did notice one thing," he said, speaking slowly. Nati had always been good about constructive criticism, and he was hoping that hadn't changed about her. "The narrative portion of your application. It's a bit…muddled."

Nati lowered her head, looking up at him through long brown eyelashes. "I might be responsible for that. You know how bad my writing can be."

Of course. Her struggles with dyslexia came with a side of dysgraphia, making her handwriting an adventure to interpret.

"It's not the handwriting, though I clearly haven't lost the ability to interpret it. No, it's not focused. Your committee will have access to the kind of information you shared with me today, but a compelling narrative laying out your needs in an organized way can push your application over the line into winning territory."

Nati pulled over the folder, scanning the pages. "I could rewrite it."

"If you'd like," he continued, his heart somewhere in his throat, "I could revise it for you. I've written a few grant proposals, though my father would be the expert." He smiled at the image of a much younger Papá receiving news that he'd been awarded one of the grants from a proposal he'd written. "He'd love to help you out. It would give him something to do besides listen to music, waiting for his next chemo appointment."

Nati's set down the folder, staring at him. "You would do that?"

"I would."

She drummed her fingers against the folder, Another one of her tics. He hadn't actively thought of them lately, but seeing her tap her pencil or bounce her leg provoked other, older memories of her doing the same.

Nati's mind appeared lost in some calculation or other.

At length, she said. "Okay. I would have to talk to Caleb and Tahira to get their okay, but until then, it's a tentative yes."

"Fair enough."

Nati bit her lip. "But I don't think they're going to mind. We can use all the help we can get. We only have so many resources." Nati gave a small laugh. "We need to win this grant."

Leo nodded. "I always wanted to do something like this. If I can help in any way, even with just revising this part of the application, I am happy to do so."

"Thank you," she said, and there was so much sincerity in her words, it did things to Leo's breathing.

"Val is opening a new Navarro's. Did you know that?" she said suddenly.

Leo started from his thoughts. "Caleb might have mentioned it."

Nati rubbed her hands together, almost in glee. "Val's grand opening coincides with a neighborhood block party taking place this weekend. We decided to do a fundraiser for the clinic, also. She's donating ten percent of the receipts for the night, which Wagner Developments will match."

"The same family that Val married into."

"Yes."

Leo blinked at that information. "Anyone else would have tried to leverage that kind of influence."

Nati sucked her teeth, a decidedly unprofessional act that nevertheless charmed Leo. Her slow relaxation in his company was like fresh air, and he didn't want to do anything to interfere with it. "That's not how we were raised. The Navarros come by their successes honestly. I don't want any questions of impropriety, not when it comes to my clinic. We win or we lose on our merits, not because we happened to marry into wealth."

Leo thought about his mother and her characterization of Nati as an impoverished, ambitious girl only interested in social mobility through marriage to the

Espinozas. He really wished his mother could hear Nati now.

Nati lifted her chin, though the smirk she repressed was not entirely serious. "Anyway, the event is a good example of what we do in the community to help the clinic. The local newspapers will be at the festival, and as I understand it, reservations are booked up for opening night. You remember my cousin Olivia, right?"

How could Leo forget? Olivia was a force of nature. "Yeah. She threatened to hack into my life if I hurt you in any way."

The curls that sprang lose from Nati's ponytail bounced with her laughter. "That sounds like her. Anyway, she's handling the social media campaign for both Val's restaurant and my fundraiser. We're setting up a donation table for people attending the block party who want to give money directly." She paused, and if he hadn't known better, he would have thought she was nervous. "You could…come. You could check out the fundraiser. And I think my family would love to say hello to you."

Ah, only for that. But it was an opening, and Leo would take it. "Okay. I'll definitely come out. I just need the time and place."

Nati jerked to attention. Maybe she'd thought he wouldn't accept. "Right." She pulled her handbag out of the bottom desk drawer and fished out a flyer. "This gives you all the details. Like I said, it's by reservation, and it's already packed, but you can keep me company at the donation table."

"Thank you."

Nati shrugged, resting her cheek in her hand. "I happen to have an in with the owner."

"I bet you do," Leo said, mirroring her actions. Her eyes flicked quickly over him, but nothing about her position changed. Yet the inexorable pull toward her was proving difficult to keep in check.

"Like you said. East Ward's changed a lot. Prepare yourself."

"I'm looking forward to seeing how it's changed.

"Do you still mix drinks as a hobby?" Nati asked suddenly, and Leo liked this. Liked the way she remembered things, how she was interested in him beyond whatever feedback he could give her on her project proposal.

"Yeah. In fact, I promised Caleb I'd make dinner on Sunday." Leo tilted his head to gaze at Nati. "What if I made dinner for all of you? You, Caleb and Tahira. You'll be wiped out after your sister's grand opening the night before."

"And work. I have an early shift on Sunday."

"Perfect." Leo straightened up, his body coursing with excitement. "We can relax like we used to."

Nati considered him, and for the thousandth time, he wished he could figure out what was going on in her mind. People thought that because Nati was happy and upbeat, she was also transparent. But that had never been the case with Nati. She was bright and cheerful, but she always played her cards close to her chest.

She nodded finally and said, "Okay. But be prepared. Tahira is going to expect you to do some serious sucking up. She likes a good, wholehearted grovel straight from the heart…or the wallet." Nati said this with a small smile, and it made Leo's whole day. God, he hadn't realized until that moment just how hungry he was for any little sliver of warmth she offered him.

"How about straight from the kitchen. It's going to be an extra-special meal, and she's always loved good food," Leo said.

Nati, who was fidgeting with bits of salad from the club sandwich she'd ordered, paused without looking up. "You're right. Tahira hasn't changed at all. None of us have, really. I think that's the thing that will surprise you the most."

Leo wasn't surprised, not when he considered himself. Yes, he had experience and was a bit wiser. But fundamentally, he was the same Leo who, every time he looked at Nati, wanted to walk up to her, place his hands on her hips and pull her flush against him. As it was, he could only imagine her heat, the ghost of her skin against his, and sit there, miserable and unsatisfied. Those feelings for her, he was coming to realize, hadn't changed after all.

"Thank you for the tour," he said quietly.

"Well," she said, lifting her head to shake out curls that were tied tight in a bun, an old tic that he was thrilled to find she still possessed. "It wasn't the worst thing ever."

"A rousing recommendation. I appreciate that."

Nati let a small laugh escape, the smile that lingered feeding his hungry soul. "Happy to oblige."

Leo smoothed the front of his shirt, his own nervous habit that he caught too late, and glanced at the clock. Best to make his escape, now that they were on a high note. "I'll get going. See you on Saturday?"

"Saturday," Nati answered quietly, the expression on her face soft, almost wistful, and he wanted to bask in it, wanted to feel her warmth melt all the way through him for the first time in years. And the way she leaned into him made him think that maybe these years had been long and cold for her, too. The better man in him hoped that wasn't true, but the more selfish Leo, the Leo that still wanted her after all these years, hoped that those years had been as dreary for her as they'd been for him. Maybe then they could melt the ice of those empty days together.

Chapter Nine

Nati

Nati had been busy the last couple of weeks, so she had not seen Val's final touches on the restaurant. When she and Olivia arrived at the restaurant on the afternoon of the opening, they stood at the swinging doors of the kitchen, taking in the dining room. It was stunning, recalling the lush, warm influences of the island together with the spare grace and elegance of a city eatery.

"Looks good all put together like this," Olivia whispered.

They were surrounded by wooden beams and floor, mosaic accents, walls painted the palest yellow that called to mind the villas of the south of Puerto Rico.

Nati had recalled it being open and airy during the day, but in the evening, with electric lanterns casting a golden glow, the restaurant pulsed as if the venue had swallowed candlelight. Val had once told her that she'd never forgotten the restaurant Philip had taken her on their first date and wanted to recreate that warm glow. Plants and flowering trees adorned the corners of the room, bringing the tropical forest indoors, and Nati almost expected the cry of the coqui or the flutter of hummingbirds to fill the air. If she let her imagination roam, she would no longer be in a restaurant but in a land of myth that recalled the stories her mother told her when she was young.

An unbidden memory came to the fore of Nati's mind. Leo's nickname for her. He used to call her *mi colibri*, or my hummingbird, because of the way she went from one thing to the next with boundless energy. Her brain had somehow hidden those memories from her, perhaps as a coping mechanism, but now they exploded into her consciousness, a cascade of moments when Leo had referred to her by a nickname only they knew and understood. Every context surged to life—the flush of new love, the domestic day-to-day of lives circumscribed by responsibilities, the heat of unrestrained abandon. And in every one, his words for her were the same:

Mi colibri. My hummingbird. La mujer de mi vida.

If Nati didn't stop, that well of emotion she kept stoppered through sheer will and distraction would come undone, rendering her unrecognizable to herself and everyone around her.

Game face. It was family time.

Thankfully, Val emerged from the kitchen, giving Nati something else to think about. Her chef's outfit was stylish and clean, her thick curly hair tied back, the angles of her face immaculately made up. Their mother's rosary, which Val never left home without, winked at Nati from the valley of her sister's button-up. "What do you think? Caio did a wonderful job with the wood, didn't he?"

Caio was one of Rosario's cousins, and the owner of Aguardiente, a local club/restaurant that served as the social center of the community. In addition to pitching in to help Rosario as a bouncer a few nights a week, he owned a local small home-renovation company. The Navarros been going to Caio for years. It would have been inconceivable for Val to go to anyone else for the renovation of the restaurant space. That's how this community worked. They supported and built each other up.

"He outdid himself," Olivia said, unable to hold back the awe in her voice.

"Makes the original look like a diner," Nati added.

Val's breath rattled out of her and she blinked rapidly, chasing away the brightness in her eyes. "This was always my dream, you know? To run a place where I could experiment and create meals for people who want to try something different. But it will never replace Mami and Papi's place."

Mami and Papi. As if Mami hadn't left. Dammit. If Val kept this up, Nati was going to cry for real.

She did the usual and squashed those feelings down.

"I'm proud of you, *hermana*," Nati said, giving her a hug. "Mami would have loved it, too."

When Val pulled back, she gave Nati a kiss on the cheek. "Thank you."

Nati nodded, then to break the heavy mood, she said, "I'm taking up my station at the donation table outside. People traffic is going to be heavy, and I have to catch those dollars. Olivia will be taking the pictures for the Instagram page. So you get Olivia's free labor tonight."

"Oh, please. She gets my free labor all the time. You would think a Navarro wouldn't know what a payable wage is. We should unionize," Olivia quipped, her voice a little thick with a feeling she was also trying to suppress.

"She can pay me in food," Nati laughed.

"Callate," Val snapped, the heavy mood dissipating, giving way to the usual give and take that characterized Navarro relationships. "The ten percent of proceeds that I'm donating tonight is payment enough, pest."

"I am not a pest." Nati gave her usual refrain.

"And the donation to the clinic actually has nothing to do with me, so where's mine?" Olivia said, crossing her arms.

"You get a piece of the cake we are serving for dessert to celebrate the grand opening." Val handed Olivia an elegant apron with the gold letters of the restaurant's name and logo emblazoned along the front. "Put this on. I need to finish up in the back."

Nati rolled her eyes as Olivia huffed dramatically,

but it was all for show. There was no question that they answered each other's calls for help when needed. And tonight was a huge night for Val. Of course, they were going to show up for her.

"Hey, at least she doesn't have you standing in as a bartender, and a really bad one at that," Rafi's voice came from behind them. He was stationed at the bar, bottles and glasses glittering around him like pirate gold. "Her bartender had a fender bender on the way here and is going to be late. I don't know the first thing about making drinks."

"Where's Papi?" Nati interjected quickly before Rafi got lost in his rant.

Rafi waved his hand as if the question was of minimal importance. "He's probably in the kitchen with Val. He's the only one who can go back there without getting his head bitten off. This doesn't solve my problem! I'm not qualified to be back here."

Olivia shrugged. "Customers are probably just going to ask for wine or soft drinks. It's not Aguardiente," Aguardiente was the center of social life in East Ward. Val's operation was a quieter one. Olivia walked round the bar, rummaging under the counter. "Here's a book of recipes for mixed drinks. You'll be okay."

"No, I will not be okay," he whined, bringing a smile to Nati's face. God, her brother was such a twelve-year-old sometimes.

"Where's the mature half of your relationship?" Nati asked.

"Mature," Rafi muttered before answering. "Étienne's flying in later tonight. He can't save me.

How the hell do you make a freaking flaming orange old fashioned?"

"You're actually assuming someone's going to ask for a flaming orange old fashioned? Come on, Rafi," Nati said, stepping out of the way of a server wheeling a rolling cart with cutlery and plates to set the tables. "You'll be fine. And anyway, how long will it take this guy to get here?"

Rafi threw up his hands in despair. *"¡No se!"*

Nati chuckled, giving him a sympathetic pat on the shoulder before walking away, looking for some way to be useful, since her table would take all of ten minutes to set up. She'd been helping in her father's restaurant since she was a little girl, running between her mother's and sister's legs in the kitchen, escaping Rafi's clutches and getting constantly scooped up by her father. She couldn't cook to save her life and had spent much of her childhood being scolded for care-lessness in the kitchen, with its boiling pots and hot ovens. Despite that, however, she had managed to pick up some basic skills.

But the grand opening wasn't making her anxious. She could handle that. It was the prospect of seeing Leo. She had invited him, after all, and no matter how many times she told herself it was all part of work-ing with her on her proposal, she couldn't help the ex-citement that came with knowing she would see him again. It was purgatory to have him near her, to have to engage with him as a friend, when every single part of her seemed to have forgotten that years and years had passed and she was not allowed to want him. She occupied a reality that constantly took her back to a time of their not-so-friendly competitions over grades and accolades, of secret kisses that turned into much more, the period of her life when her body would come alive like an electrical charge every time he was near. She was not a medical student anymore. She was a full adult, an attending physician and the cofounder of a community clinic. Leo was a man who'd lived an entire life, a life that hadn't included her.

Nati decided that getting out of the restaurant and setting up her table after all might take her mind off Leo. She invoked that powerful concentration that had served her time and again in her life. She always visualized herself as unbreakable, made of steel. There wasn't one thing she couldn't achieve if she put her incredible faculties to the task of chasing it down. She was going to collect those donations like a boss and kick that squatter out of her brain.

Nati paused and burst out into a fit of hysterical giggles that drew the eyes of those walking close to her side off the sidewalk. She really went in that hard to keep Leo out of her mind.

Still chortling to herself, she focused on smiling and waving people she knew over to her table. Music from a band at the end of the street filled the night, while kids ran between food carts and stands selling local crafts and preserved foods. People stood in clusters throughout the street to eat and chat. It was the kind of energy that Nati thrived on.

She had just finished a conversation with one of the

older residents when Val's husband, Philip, arrived. Val met him at the entrance greeting him with a quick kiss.

"Where can I be of service?" he asked with that sweet unflappability that met Val's freneticism head on and overcame it.

Val wiped her forehead with her sleeve. "Eye candy."

Philip's face wrinkled in confusion. "Thank you, but what does that mean?"

Nati sighed. "It means you are at the host station. Help her greet customers, make sure there aren't snafus with the reservations."

Val nodded, gave him another quick kiss before disappearing inside to the kitchen again. His face was still confused. "You gathered all that from one phrase?"

"I have a lifetime of interpreting Val," Nati said, bowing slightly. "You might be the love of her life, but that kitchen right there is her kingdom, and none of us, including you, is allowed back there. So your work is out here." Val had a sous-chef and a whole setup that she'd honed to flawless perfection, and everyone except for their father was forbidden to enter. "But, you're the prettiest out of all of us, so you get to keep an eye on the front." She didn't want to say that, actually, he would help with host duty because he had no other restaurant-specific skills that they could use.

"Thank you, I think?" he said, with a sly smile that made Nati think he might have understood her thinking after all.

As guests arrived, servers trained directly by Val worked the dining room, while Nati managed her donation table and Olivia took photographs of both the crowds outside and the diners inside. Nati tried to keep a loose, mental estimate of how much the clinic would bank from the evening based on collected receipts, but she lost count somewhere after the first hour.

Despite the foot traffic, the noise and the energy of the block party, time seemed to move at a crawl until Leo materialized from the crowds at the time he'd promised. From where Nati was sitting, she allowed herself the luxury of watching Leo unawares. His walk was almost feline—contained body, careful movements that spoke of complete control. He still worked out—that was obvious, though he wasn't unnaturally buff from it. His soft gray–and–black–plaid chinos paired with a black polo and black weekend jacket looked expensive and clung deliciously to the thick muscles of his legs. The black loafers with barely-there black socks completed the outfit. He'd always loved dressing well and he hadn't lost this particular characteristic. He was good to look at.

Nati stepped up to the host stand just as the young woman was poised to turn him away. Philip had gone to show someone to their seat. "He's with me. I'll take care of him," Nati intervened.

"Perdón, Doctora Navarro." The young woman stepped away from them. Leo cast his eyes on Nati, and her mind flew to her preparations for the night, how she hadn't been able to decide on an outfit and, in the end, had opted for a red-and-orange wrap dress with matching orange pumps. It was one of the combination of colors that most suited her coloring and made her feel like a queen. And apparently, Leo seemed to

be a big fan of the outfit, because he hadn't stopped staring at her, even though he was trying to be discreet. Nati wanted to high five herself, and then scolded herself for caring at all.

"You look amazing," Leo said, a little breathless.

Nati waved her hand. "Aww, this old thing?" She couldn't help the laugh that erupted at the absurd comment, and to her pleasure, he followed suit.

"Doesn't look old," Leo said, surveying her appreciatively, which just added to his audacity and the general overheating of Nati's skin. If it had been anyone else letting his thirst hang out like that, she might have had something to say. But this was Leo and Leo was—

"You look really good, too," she answered, unable to entirely keep the tremor out of her voice. The sudden desire to reach over, take a nip out of the skin exposed by the open collar, spread a possessive hand over the muscles of his forearm, pull him in and squeeze hard made her take a step back.

Leo nodded, running an unconscious thumb over his bottom lip that had Nati swaying slightly. "Want a drink?"

"I would love—oh, maybe not." She recovered quickly when she craned her head inside the entrance of the restaurant and caught Rafi's deer-in-headlights expression. "Oh, boy. Okay, follow me." She led Leo inside, weaving between two parties of four who were waiting for a table. She arrived at the bar just in time to hear Rafi speaking to the waitress.

"I understand. I'm sorry I messed up his margarita," he hissed. "Tell him I'll make him something else. Maybe a rum and Coke?

"Rafi?" Nati said, causing him to jerk to a start.

"Nati? Hey, yeah, I got a customer complaining that I made his margarita wrong. I did everything the recipe book told me to do, and look." He put the drink on the counter, the umbrella shoved into the ice looking soggy and wilted. Nati picked it up, took a whiff of it, and put it down, coughing as the vapors hit her nose.

"How much tequila did you put in that thing?" Nati said, blinking the tears from her eyes. She pushed it toward Leo. His reaction, more subdued, was also one of revulsion.

"I used the measuring cup. Look." Rafi pulled out a shot glass. An entire shot glass.

"That's twice the size of a jigger," Leo said. "May I?"

Rafi's attention swiveled to Leo, the panic clearly making him completely disconnected from what was happening around him because his next words were "Dr. Sabroso?"

"*¿Que?*" Nati and Leo said in unison.

Rafi's face went pale. "I…oh…sorry. I meant to say… Well, I don't know what I meant to say. Just not that."

Oh, god. Nati wanted to crawl under the counter and lie alongside any dead cockroaches that had beaten her to the afterlife. Rafi was incapable of telling a credible lie, and she was currently benefiting from his rare and useless talent.

"I'm actually good at mixing drinks," Leo said good-naturedly. "It was a hobby of mine when I was in college."

Rafi's eyes grew wide, and he was out from behind the bar and next to his sister and Leo with a speed Nati hadn't believed him capable of. "You know how to mix drinks?" he whispered, as desperate as Gollum staring Frodo down for the One Ring.

"Yeah, that's what I was saying."

Rafi took off his apron and threw it over Leo's head. "I'll clear tables."

"Rafi!" Nati practically shouted, remembering herself in time to lower her voice. "Leo can't just go back there and mix drinks." He'd just gotten there, and she had barely had a chance to talk to him.

"If our dear sister can station a complete incompetent like me back there, he can mix drinks. You offered, right?"

"I did," Leo said, suppressing a laugh.

Rafi waved at the counter. "It's all yours." He leaned in close to him. "Save me."

Leo nodded solemnly, the corner of his lips quirking slightly. "I got this."

To Nati's utter amazement, Leo took his station behind the bar and proceeded to prepare a margarita in the time it would have taken Rafi to flip through the recipe book and gather the ingredients. Rafi's natural tendency toward perfectionism and precision had probably rendered him incapable of preparing anything with a speed that was remotely appropriate to the venue. Soon, drink requests were coming fast and furious, and Leo handled them with extraordinary finesse. Nati shouldn't have been as impressed as she was—it wasn't the first time she'd seen Leo whip up a party's worth of drinks, lingering for the inevitable praise that came as a result of his creations, praise he basked in. But he came off much more confident than he had as a college kid playing at bartending, especially in his expensive dinner wear.

"Your bartender's not coming, is he?" Nati asked Val when she came out to survey the dining area.

Val shook her head, distressed. "No, he had to go because the EMTs on the scene said he had a concussion. Poor guy. He only just started."

"If he'd come in while I was on shift, I might have treated him."

"So glad you weren't," Val said, giving her a hug. "I need you here. While you owe me an explanation for the sudden appearance of your ex, do you think Leo might want to stick it out for the last couple of hours? I'll pay him the going rate."

"Hey, you'll pay him but not me?" Rafi approached, unable to keep the petulance out of his voice.

"You nearly poisoned your customers!" Nati exclaimed.

"Not poisoned. Not poisoned at all. Just put in a little too much liquor," Rafi huffed indignantly.

"You get love," Val said. "That's what you get. But Dr. Sabroso here—"

"You see, it's not just me!" Rafi said, fist pumping into the air. "I have been vindicated."

Nat rolled his eyes. "I'll talk to him, but I'm pretty sure he doesn't want your money."

Val leaned in, all cloying sweetness that promised nothing good. "Maybe you could find your own way to thank him."

"What?" Nati gasped.

Rafi guffawed at her expression. "Not you up to your matchmaking ways, big sister?"

Val elbowed him. "Worked for you, didn't it?"

"You two are annoying as hell, you know that?" Nati growled, thankful that at least Olivia was too busy terrorizing people into posing for her photographs to tease Nati as well.

"Quid pro quo, baby." Rafi chortled with glee. Ungrateful brat.

Nat turned on her heel, left her meddlesome siblings behind and made her way to the bar, dodging servers like a ping-pong ball to arrive where Leo was pouring out two glasses of red wine. He pushed one toward her and held the other in his hand.

"A toast," he said, raising his glass.

Nati clinked her glass against his, swirling the liquid to release its aroma before taking a sip. It was good. Full bodied, smoky aftertaste with a touch of something like anise. "What are we toasting?"

Leo tilted his head to the side. "Starting over."

"You're moving back to East Ward?" Nati asked.

Leo gave her a thoughtful look. "I haven't planned that far ahead yet. Right now, I'm taking it day by day with my father. But I'm on my way to making amends with my friends. With you. That counts for something."

Nati leaned against the counter, the soothing notes

of alcohol flowing through her, loosening her up. "Maybe when you're done with your shift tonight, I know a place we can hang out."

Leo raised an eyebrow. "Your bartender isn't showing, is he?"

Nati felt guilt wash over her at wasting his evening this way. "Would you mind? Val said she'd pay you."

He swirled his glass of wine, staring at the vortex created by the rich liquid. "Consider it part of the donation to your clinic fundraiser." He accepted an order from one of the servers and pulled up two bottles of beer, uncapping them and setting them on the bar. "And I'm definitely taking you up on hanging out afterward."

"I did offer."

Leo laughed, and Nati couldn't help but notice his freshly trimmed beard. She imagined the warm scrape of it against her skin, the patch of red it would leave behind. Running her fingers up his sideburns into his thick hair. "Where do you want to go? I noticed the place where we used to hang out, The Wild Wolf, is still in business."

"You read my mind! That's exactly where I was going to suggest we go."

Leo's smile was mischievous and bright, and Nati was no longer in her sister's restaurant surrounded by the hustle of a newly opened business. She was somewhere in the past, remembering one of the many times she and Leo had gone out to unwind, or met up with Tahira and Caleb just to hang out. Their aimless conversations, how they could talk about nothing for hours. How holding each other's hand across a table made conversation unnecessary because they understood each other so well.

She couldn't help but wonder if it had been the same with his ex-wife. If that was why Nati had been so easy to forget, because what had seemed so powerful, so uniquely theirs, had been easy to find elsewhere. Maybe it was a mistake to believe it had ever existed, or to imagine that it might exist again.

Another order came through, and Leo made quick work of it. Nati really needed to get back to her table. She hadn't been planning to stay until closing, but a couple more hours at her donation table might bring in more funds for the clinic. At least, that was the excuse she was going with.

"Okay?" she asked when he'd handed off drinks to the server.

"Okay." Leo lifted his glass to clink against Nati's again. "It's a date."

Nati flipped her hair over her shoulder—a queen's move, if she said so herself. "I'll pick you up when the bar closes."

Leo nodded, his smile trailing behind her as she made her way outside the restaurant and to her table. Even with the bustle of movement around the restaurant, Nati could have sworn, even when she couldn't see him any longer, that she could still feel his smile on her.

Chapter Ten

Leo

It wasn't how Leo had expected to spend his Saturday night—making drinks and wiping down a strange bar during its grand opening. But he wasn't sorry. He hadn't been called on to make that many drinks since he was in college and he had enjoyed it as much as he had then. A big part of the pleasure came from being praised for doing something well. He always knew he had a bit of a praise kink, and he liked nothing more than to hear how much people liked his work.

But the look on Nati's face when she thanked him, as if he were some superhero, flying in to save the day? Her appreciation satisfied every single one of his cravings and made him feel ten feet tall. And Nati had always been good about giving him positive feedback and letting him know how happy he made her. He felt the renewed thrill of hearing words like those come from her again. There was nothing he could do; she was always going to pull those desires from him, turn around and satisfy them. And he was always going to want to make her happy.

"Ready?" he asked when she'd packed up the table.

Nati bit back a yawn but nodded. "Thanks. It seems you are my official rescuer tonight." She paused and glanced up at him from under her long brown lashes. "You did really well."

Her praise sent a thrill of electricity up and down his spine. "Thank you." They stepped out onto the boulevard, the crowds of earlier still going strong as they finished dinner, and walked along the avenue, heading for their old hangout to spend the remainder of their evening. The night was still warm, and he caught Nati fanning herself with one of the fundraiser flyers.

"Do you remember Santos's party? That long weekend we had during our third year?" She tapped her chin, as if to shake the memory free.

"You mean the one where he mixed piña colada in an actual tub and used the oar from his father's canoe to stir it?"

"Yes," Nati chuckled, raising a finger in sudden illumination. "It was in March. I remember because the St. Patrick's Day parade happened about five days later."

Nati had always possessed a wicked memory for dates, able to remember even the most obscure events by relating them to something else. "I always thought it was scary how good you are at remembering dates."

"Well," Nati said, a self-satisfied grin on her face at the compliment. "You have your bartending superpowers, and I have super date-recall powers. The universe couldn't grant all her gifts to one person."

"Oh, absolutely not. What was I thinking?" Leo said, reveling in their banter. "How lucky to have gotten the most useful superpower imaginable."

"It was useful tonight." She smiled, lifting her face into a breeze that shimmered over them. He and Nati had done this entire strip together when they were younger. They were alike in that way. There was nothing they'd loved more than to try new restaurants, join the local trivia nights or just socialize in a bar. They both loved to meet and talk to people, loved the bustle of bodies, of good food and music. It made being with Nati easy because she had never been a dull date.

They entered The Wild Wolf, the mood as mellow as the saxophone player on the small stage. People sat in clusters on leather sofas, at tall bar tables with endless legs, on cushioned benches or simply stood in groups, talking as the music played. Though close to closing, the kitchen served them a mixed antipasto platter and crusty baguette bread.

"Bet it's more fun when someone else is doing the mixing," Nati said, pouring out the Sanbitter in a glass and taking a sip of the red liquid.

He clinked glasses against hers. "I could do it all night. But when with company, I prefer to let someone else handle the drinks."

Nati smiled at this, smoothing out her dress, clearly enjoying the atmosphere. Leo ignored the humming under his skin, the latent tension that pulled every muscle tight, making him hyperaware of Nati's presence. He wanted to relax, watch people and enjoy the evening in the way he loved most, but Nati needled at his awareness, making him vigilant, as if he were waiting for something to happen.

"I wanted to thank you again for helping out tonight," she said without warning.

Leo waved it away. "It was nothing. Really." He set his empty glass down and rested his hands over his leg. "Even though we aren't…" He waved a finger between them, then let out a burst of air that was pure exasperation directed at himself. "I just mean, your family was always good to me. How could I not help?"

"Even Rafi?" Nati teased, taking a sip of her drink. Between them was her crossed leg and heeled sandal bouncing slightly as they spoke. Leo's eyes flickered to the manicured toes, a glittering sienna that flowed smoothly with the color of her skin, the swell of calf pushed out from the pressure against the other leg. He was admiring her a bit at a time, taking in pieces of her, which his mind then reorganized and slowly rebuilt into the entirety that was Nati. An entirety that filled him with an aching awareness of her. He swallowed, steadying himself against the effect she had on him.

"Even Rafi. It's his job to be the overprotective brother, and he was always very good at it." Leo laughed, recalling a few conversations they'd had when Leo had first started dating Nati.

"He was in need of saving this time, so you scored some points for that."

"Yeah. But I don't want you to spend the night thanking me," he said, leaning forward, his knee dangerously close to hers. The potential for the fabric of his pants to brush against her knee had every atom in his body on high alert. He was mere centimeters from touching her, and it was taking every ounce of strength to keep from closing that infinitesimal gap. "How are you spending your free time these days, since I have had almost one hundred percent visibility on your work life until my father was discharged?"

Nati chortled at this. "Of course you do. Everywhere I look, there you are."

"Purely unintentional. I promise."

She downed the last of her drink, and waved over a server to bring another one. "When I'm not at the hospital, I'm at the clinic. It has taken up most of my free time for the past year and a half." She spread her hands to indicate the span of time. "But it was worth it. It was one of those things I knew I'd have to accomplish in my life, and I was lucky Tahira and Caleb were ready to dive in as well."

"You were always relentless when it came to the things you wanted. Always so ambitious." His mother's words about Nati's ambition being greater than her love for him came back with a vengeance.

"I don't deny it." She sighed, as if reading his thoughts. "I don't think I've changed that much. I still like to go out, I still do yoga and take spin classes. I still spend more money than I should on clothes." She indicated her outfit. "I have more dresses than anyone with of my profession should own, and more shoes than a petty dictator's wife."

"You really haven't changed one bit, then, because that's always been you." Leo shook his head.

"Not at all, I'm remarkably consistent, as my brother never fails to remind me. How about you?"

Uncertainty washed over him. Had he changed? He certainly wasn't as naive as he had once been, but neither was he the heartbroken young man of before, forced to abandon the one person he'd been convinced was his soulmate. He'd moved on to another stage, where pain became nostalgia and loss became memory, something he simply carried around as a part of him.

"Six years is a lot. I'd like to think I haven't changed either, but maybe *evolved* is the better word."

"*Evolved* is a very good word." Her eyes fell to her lap, and suddenly she was the shy, uncertain one. "Why don't you tell me what you've been up to all these years?"

Leo shrugged. "I went to California for that residency, as you know, and ended up staying."

She sat stiffly but listened, hands clasped tightly on her lap.

"My mother came and stayed with me for a little while. A very little while." He shook his head at that. "My mother is better in small doses."

"Amen to that," Nati said, raising a glass. Leo

clinked his glass with hers. He couldn't be offended when it was the absolute truth. She took a gulp, a rather large one, then added, "What else?"

What else, what else? "I started my residency at UCLA's Medical Center. It was everything you said it would be, remember?" Leo felt the shadow of the past on him. Nati had told him years ago how great the hospital was, the prestigious surgeons he'd be working with, how impossible their relationship would become in a situation like that because he would barely have time to breathe, much less call and Zoom and visit her. Her final argument—that she simply didn't love him enough to go through that—came back to him in all its three dimensions, and he shoved away the awful feeling of loss it provoked in him.

"And then you got married," Nati said quietly. The saxophonist finished his set, the conversation becoming a dull lull in the background, and Nati, the Nati who'd been laughing and taunting earlier, had disappeared behind the mask she'd worn the first day he'd come to see her present at the clinic. "Tell me about that."

Leo shrugged. "I met Michelle through my family. My mother, actually."

"Playing Cupid. Of course." Nati huffed out a laugh, but it fell heavy and humorless between them.

When she said no more, he continued. "It was a fast courtship. We just hit it off." Like his mother had said they would. She knew him well enough to know who might be interesting to him, at least. "We have a lot in common, and she's a very kind person. She's still my friend to this day. We just weren't marriage material." That, despite the fact that he'd desperately wanted them to be marriage material. He'd wanted someone to be his, someone who wouldn't just up and abandon him. He'd wanted to pull together the fractured pieces of his heart, *to heal* after Nati, but had gone about it the wrong way.

"Guess the start of a good relationship should be a good friendship," Nati said quietly. "I'm sorry it didn't work out."

Leo lifted his hand, let it hover over her knee for a moment before pulling back. She watched him but didn't flinch. Nati had always had nerves of steel, and while he felt the entirety of his person practically shred apart, she was as placid as the surface of an ice cube. Clear, sharp and immutable.

"Friendship is important. I agree," he said. "But without passion and desire, it's like living with a roommate. For some people, that's okay. But for me, it was like living half a life, because I already knew what the alternative was like, and I couldn't live with anything less."

Nati turned away, and he felt the odd shyness of that movement. Leo was captivated all at once by the slant of her eyes, the bronze halo of her hair and the burnished gold of her skin. She was like a queen considering some important matter of state, her forefinger running a pattern over her lips. Music erupted as the saxophonist started his next set, and suddenly, Leo was awash in sensation, every single part of him awake and aware and suffused entirely by this night.

Nati had never been a quiet passion. She always came to him loud, cacophonous, overwhelming his entire person until he was deafened by her. He had gone out into the world to find what he'd once had with her, but he'd never, ever found it. That she had been the one to pull away, had taken what he'd most hungered for and starved him should have made him hesitant, should have insulated him from wanting her anymore.

He was in an emotional desert, hadn't had a drop of water in ages, and he wanted to drink and drink from her until his stomach ached and his heart and hands were full.

The difference between friendship and the way he'd once felt for Nati felt like the difference between a candle flame and a forest fire. She had once been the person he'd trusted the most, had shared everything with, including their hopes and dreams, his desire for a future, for a life with her. They *had* been friends. But what had burned between them was so much more than that, and, hungry as he was, he couldn't forget that no matter how much he'd felt for her, it still hadn't been enough to keep her from walking away.

Chapter Eleven

Nati

Nati wanted to squirm in her seat, but she didn't want to show how uncomfortable this entire conversation was making her. What sick, twisted impulse had her asking him about his marriage, of all things? To hear him tell her about the very thing that hurt her more than anything else?

"It's getting late," Nati said, finishing off the last of her drink and waving the server over. Leo reached for his wallet, but Nati put a hand up.

"You bartended for free. I've got this."

"I told you, I don't want you to pay me." Leo opened his wallet and pulled out his card.

"Is this a battle you absolutely need to win?" Nati

asked, handing her card to the server before Leo could recover from her question. "You can let a woman pay and still keep your manly rights, you know."

"I don't have a problem with a woman paying for me," he said, rubbing a hand up and down his thigh, a sign that he was nervous, but it also drew her eyes to the unflinching muscles of his thighs straining his slacks. She'd always been obsessed with his legs— strong, extremely well-shaped from years of biking, legs she had loved to touch. Nati tore her eyes away and stood abruptly, knocking an empty glass over and sending it careening toward the floor.

Leo surged forward and caught it just in time.

"That was close," he said, setting the glass on the table again.

"Sorry," Nati murmured, wanting to get out of the club with its soft music and the low chattering and *him*, *everywhere him*, as soon as possible. This was all just a painful exercise in nostalgia. Anyone would say that six years was too long to justify what was happening to her. She should not be feeling anything, and the fact that she was overwhelmed with emotion and memory told her she needed to go home as soon as possible.

"I'll probably take a cab," she said, pulling her phone out so she could access the app.

"I'm heading your way," Leo said, following her out of the bar. "We can share."

"Okay." Nati typed in the last of the information needed to obtain the car, grateful that the intensity they'd shared was slowly draining away. "Tell me about the waterfront. Does Genevieve like it? Rafi and his husband live there, too."

"I didn't know that. It's very nice. Doesn't Val's husband…?"

"Yes. It's his. He and Val live two buildings down from you." Nati paced along the sidewalk with Leo following next to her. The night was still warm though the temperature had gone down, but Nati liked the way the breeze caressed her skin.

"And Val's new restaurant? Is that also his building?"

Nati shook her head. "No. Val didn't want Philip to make this easier for her. She wanted to open that restaurant and make it work on her own, without any help."

"You Navarros never change. Just like you refusing to apply to the Wagner Foundation for funding."

"I still stand by that."

Leo let out a small chuckle. "Of course, you do. I just wanted to point out that you take after your sister much more than you realize."

Nati grew bashful. "I supposed you're right. It's hard to see myself as Val's equal since she practically raised me. Guess some of her personality rubbed off on me after all."

"She did a good job. You all did," Leo said, his voice thick, which caught Nati off-balance. The car she'd ordered pulled up, sparing Nati the need to respond. She was a tripped livewire and every nerve ending was firing at once. She had a high tolerance for adrenaline, but tonight was starting to feel like she'd come off a twelve-hour Saturday night shift in the emergency room that had had her running nonstop.

Leo held the door open as Nati slid inside, quickly entering his side of the car before closing it. Leo rested his head against the seat, watching her, which only ramped up her heart rate. Nati closed her eyes and counted to five before opening them to look at him again. "Are we okay?"

He smiled, lolling against the seat to look at her, as if they were sharing pillow talk. If Nati hadn't fortified her self-control, she would have almost reached out and kissed him. "Are we okay?" he repeated. He considered the question a few more seconds before answering. "I think we're on our way to being okay." He took a breath, poised to ask something else, which Nati waited for. Desperately. She wanted them to be more than okay. Becoming friends had seemed unattainable before. Now it didn't feel like enough.

But he didn't say anything else. Not with words. He simply stared at her, waiting. She pushed down the electric awareness of his body next to hers, the echo of his words rumbling from his chest, the dark profile that presented itself when he glanced out an even darker window, occasional lights illuminating his features. He had always been beautiful, but the beard, the close crop of auburn-brown hair, the webbed lines around his eyes that transformed his good looks into something seasoned and accessible, made it easy to imagine touching him, dragging her fingers and nails over his skin.

Nati turned away in her leather seat to look at anything but him.

"You'll come to dinner tomorrow?" he pressed.

"Yes," she answered. "I just have to—"

"—I know. Go up to the clinic and do some paperwork. I would have guessed even if you hadn't already said so."

She took the risk of looking back at him. "Because?"

"Because…" Leo reached across the space between them, sweeping a curl that stubbornly refused to stay in place and flicked it with lingering slowness behind her ear. "Nati, you haven't changed that much."

Nati's breath hitched, but she wasn't going to let a simple touch of his fingers make her lose her focus. "You would have done the same thing, if the situation were reversed."

"You see," he whispered, "how similar we still are?"

Nati's skin tingled, her lips hesitant with unearned desire.

She had forgotten the car's destination until it pulled up in front of Navarro's Family Restaurant and her apartment two floors above.

"I'll see you tomorrow." She angled her body to open the door. But Leo's hand on hers kept her from actually leaving the car.

"Thanks again for tonight," he said. When she opened her mouth to remind him that she was the one who should be thanking him, that he'd actually saved her family's behind, he stopped her by pressing a kiss to her knuckles. "Don't thank me for the bartending. That's not what I meant."

Nati's breath came out in shattered gasps, noisy and ungainly to her own ears. She worked so hard to give away as little as possible, but Leo was wearing down her hiding places and worming his way inside. The familiar brush of his lips on her skin was an assault on her composure. All the repressed yearning and missing of years and years rolled over her, threatening to flatten her. She wanted Leo, she had never stopped wanting him, and even though she'd tucked every one of those desires deep within herself, they had always been there, waiting in the darkness, waiting for the smallest opening to tumble back out again.

Careful, she warned herself.

A warning she proceeded to ignore as her body came alive with the sudden galvanizing potential that flared within the car. Leo's eyes were fixed on her, moving from her eyes to her mouth to her hair, as if he couldn't decide where his gaze should land. When it settled on her lips and lingered there, she leaned in, drawn to him, to his intensity and her desire to open up the dark places of her heart and let air and light in.

Her lips hovered over his and she paused, her eyes holding his soft green ones as she waited for him to understand that this was something she wanted, but only if he did, too. He gave a quick nod, the permission she sought to close the space that held them apart. His mouth was still the same, though the short beard was a rough contrast to the relentless softness of his lips. She pressed further and he met her, lips open, tongue gently sweeping into her mouth, the concept of time shriveling to a slow crawl in which they kissed and kissed until the driver cleared his throat.

Nati opened her eyes. It felt like coming out of a deep sleep, where everything was warm and thick and sensuous. Leo stared at her, all brooding expectation and desire. Darkness waited outside the car; the air quiet, her building looming cold and empty, and she wanted to return to the previous moment, where their kiss had held everything at bay.

She could take him upstairs. She could have this for a few hours. She could forget the past that hung like lead around their shoulders. It wouldn't be the first time she'd used sex to stand in for things she couldn't heal.

But this was Leo, and that past would follow them to the door of her bedroom and wait for them until they were sated, no matter how long that took.

She placed a hand on his chest, gentle and firm, not pulling him closer or pushing him away.

"I'll see you tomorrow, okay?" she repeated, and she hoped it didn't sound like a rejection but an invitation to wait a little longer, to wait until she had more time to get her head and her heart on the same page.

Leo cupped Nati's chin, his thumb tracing a line across her bottom lip. "Good night, *colibiri*."

She slid her hand behind his neck and sank her head into the crook of his neck, the heat of his arms sliding to hold her in turn. He released a tiny grunt and a sigh that reverberated through her body. *Don't say a word*, she wanted to beg as she held him, letting the moment flutter through her like a pair of rapidly beating wings. She inhaled him, pinioning him to her chest until she was no longer at risk of coming apart. She pulled back then and held his gaze briefly once more before turning to open the door and slipping out of the car on light feet, heart racing a thousand beats per minute as she dashed across the pavement.

If only she could trust this; if only it was more than just the comfort and longing for a thing long past. If only she could be sure this was real. She might let herself have this again. Then she would fly away on pure emotion, like a bird finally released from captivity.

Chapter Twelve

Leo

It had taken Leo forever to fall asleep, streaks of dawn dispelling his thoughts and allowing him to finally rest. It was barely a few stolen moments in the back of a Lyft, but Nati's kiss had been like a homecoming and a blow to his chest.

Ay dios mío.

Leo rested his elbows on counter of his sister's kitchen island, the jolt of three espressos in a row buzzing through his brain fog. He was buried up to his knuckles in hair, pulling hard in the hopes that the pain would provide him the clarity he needed. If he'd ever suffered from an undiagnosed arrhythmia, this would have been the perfect moment for his heart to give out.

Nati had kissed him. Hot and long and full of all the knowledge she'd once had of him together with a newfound sense of confidence, as if she could calculate the effect each twist of lip and tongue might have on him. That kiss would leave an imprint he would remember for the rest of his life.

But she'd also broken his heart, and he struggled to reconcile these two facts into something he could believe in. He was a nauseating mix of hope and fear, and he didn't know where to place himself.

The sound of a key inserting into the lock of the apartment door startled him out of his thoughts. Genevieve stepped inside, removing her light jacket, a buttoned indigo shirt half-tucked into a pair of relaxed-fit jeans. She started when she stepped into the kitchen and saw Leo.

"You scared me!" she exclaimed.

Leo looked at the clock, noticing that it was earlier than he'd thought. He really was running on next to no sleep. "I thought I was meeting you at Mamá's house."

"I thought Mamá was busy this morning, but she wasn't, so I decided to come home and check on you." Genevieve crossed the space to the coffee maker, frowning at the empty pot. "You used the mini espresso bar?"

Leo nodded, still nursing the tiny espresso cup.

She made an indistinct noise and set out to make a cup of regular coffee. "Should I make some of this for you, too? Or are you maxed out with the espressos?"

Leo moaned, leaning his heads in his hands. "I'm maxed out, but I think I'll take it anyway."

Genevieve pinched her lip, taking him in, no doubt horrified by his exhausted appearance. "Late night?"

"A little."

She sniffed before preparing the coffee maker and setting it to brew. "What were you up to that had you out so late?"

Leo looked up at his sister, debating on what to say, then opted for the truth. "I went to the grand opening of Val's new restaurant."

His sister, who had pulled two mugs out of the cabinet and set them gently on the counter between them, asked, "Was Nati a part of this visit?"

He rubbed his hands down his face, feeling every crease and jowl. "Very much a part of the visit."

Genevieve bit her lip, then gave a genuine squeal of delight. "Are you guys…?"

"Don't get carried away." he practically growled. Why hadn't anyone ever warned him that emotional hangovers could be just as bad as physical ones?

"Did you have fun, at least?" Genevieve asked, the coffee machine sputtering its last drops. She poured two cups, passed the sugar and cream and took the stool across from him.

"I did." He stared at his coffee, the steam mesmerizing as it swirled off the surface.

"Helloooo?" Genevieve said, tapping his cup with a spoon. "That coffee isn't going to fix itself."

He dropped his head between his shoulder blades, lightly tapping the table with his forehead. "Gen, what the hell am I doing?" He looked up, scooping two heaping spoons of sugar into his coffee. "I had. An amazing. Time."

"With Nati."

He nodded. "With Nati."

"And you're pressed."

"Extremely pressed."

She took the spoon away just as he was going to add the third mountain of sugar. "And you're freaked out because she broke up with you out of left field and you can't be certain she won't do it again."

Leo looked up at her with something like awe. "How do you do that?"

Genevieve rolled her eyes. "It is literally the plot of one of my novels." She looked in askance at his coffee cup. "Are you really trying to drink that sludge?"

Leo pushed it toward her. "Think I've had enough. Gen…" He spread his hands, trying to convey his utter and total helplessness.

"It's a risk. I've always liked Nati and I never thought her to be fickle, but that was a strange moment in your lives. You were going in two separate directions. Few relationships would have survived that."

"She didn't even try."

Genevieve sighed. "That was a long time ago. You were a lot younger and had a lot going against you. Circumstances are different now."

"How? I live all the way across the country."

"That's what U-Hauls are for. Papá would get up out of his sick bed and make a party if you moved back home."

"And Mamá?"

"Mamá?" Genevieve laughed. "She has some nerve criticizing Nati for being too ambitious when she would be all too happy to have you on the moon if it meant she could brag about your amazing job. Pot calling the kettle black is what that is." At Leo's blank stare, Genevieve said, "You really aren't good at connecting the dots, are you? People often despise in others the faults they perceive in themselves. Ever wonder why Mamá and Papá aren't married, even though they obviously love each other?"

"I wouldn't put that all on Mom," Leo said. "I remember the arguments."

"I'm not saying it's all on Mamá, but I would also say it's not all on Papá, either." Genevieve sighed. "They got hung up on things and never let them go. Just don't you go doing the same thing. Now drink up. I'm going to pick up a few things for Papá and you can keep me company."

"I'm terrible company," Leo complained.

"So?" She gave him a smirk that took him back to when they were still young and constantly annoyed with each other. "I just need somebody to carry my things."

After Leo accompanied his sister to visit with his father, leaving her to spend the night with their parents, Leo settled in to plan the evening. Cooking took Leo's mind off his conversation with his sister. It was good to finally do something that involved the part of his brain that was not drowning in worry. Leo wasn't the best cook in the world, but he enjoyed the full engagement it required. Like when he performed a surgery, he was fully invested in the moment, allowing a quieter part of his brain to work on his problems in the background.

He was lucky to have had friends from many different backgrounds. But cooking for a diverse group such as Caleb, Tahira and Nati would be a challenge. He wouldn't go for Latin cuisine—Nati had always served up excellent Puerto Rican food from her sister's restaurants, and Caleb's parents were both amazing cooks, ruling out both Dominican and Southern Black cuisine. Indian food was out of the question for the same reasons. He wasn't going to set himself up for a negative comparison.

So he went for something that was beyond all their culinary comfort zones and tried for a Thai meal. Leo made note of his friend's allergies—Nati and watermelon, Caleb and shellfish, Tahira and lactose—and settled on a menu of khao soi soup, steamed lime fish and vegetables, jasmine rice and sticky rice for dessert.

He had a lot of ground to cover with Caleb and Tahira. He'd essentially abandoned them after his breakup with Nati and would have to work hard to get them to fully trust him again. Forming friendships when people were younger was always so much easier than when people were older, and in many ways, it was like starting new again.

That evening, Tahira arrived first, handing him a large, heavy ceramic bowl covered in aluminum foil. Leo lifted the edge, taking a peek inside, and was assaulted by the aromas that escaped in billowy puffs of vapor. "Mmm, couscous," he said.

"Couscous and seven vegetables. Because I remember how much you like meat and knew we would all be desperate for something green."

"Ahaa!" Leo said. "I still love meat, but I have also learned to live with vegetables."

"Salad does not count," she sniffed, hanging her bag on a peg in the hallway. She adjusted her headscarf, wrapping the gorgeous blue-and-magenta material before tucking it up.

"Steamed vegetables in lime sauce," he retorted, carrying the bowl to the kitchen, where she followed.

"Look at you, growing and evolving. Maybe there is hope for you yet."

"Some of us do get better with time."

"Hard to know when you do all that changing far away from your friends." She put her hands on her hips, her mood shifting so quickly, Leo wondered if emotional whiplash was a verifiable condition. "But now that you are here, you will hear me now before everyone else arrives. You hurt me."

He turned away from the counter, facing her. "Tahira," he said pitifully, but she wasn't finished with him. Not by a long shot.

"Not only me, but Caleb as well. I cannot believe that after everything we went through—everything you and Caleb went through—you did not rate us highly enough as friends to stay connected when things ended between you and Nati. Caleb will not dwell on it because he is too sweet and too forgiving, but I am not. You owe us—*me*—an explanation." Her deep, lilting voice cracked, and she swallowed hard before continuing. "How could you?"

"Tahira, I don't know what to tell you. I wasn't in a good place after Nati ended things and I… I couldn't take any reminders of her. Especially when I first left."

"But you got married, Leo! You got into a whole marriage not six months later. You cannot have been suffering that much if you were with someone else. And yet you sent no invitations, you made no contact. Nothing. It was as if we never existed. If you were able to get married to another woman, start a whole new life, surely it meant you were not in such a bad place anymore, right?"

Leo dropped his eyes and didn't answer because whatever he said would make him look like either a liar or a fool. And while he could admit to being the biggest fool on the planet, he refused to lie to his friend.

He snuck a glance at Tahira and watched the slow spread of understanding overtake her features. "Oh, Leo. Please tell me you did not do what I think you did."

"Don't say anything to Nati. She doesn't need to know."

"You mean, don't tell her that you never got over her? That you married another woman thinking that was the solution to your heartbreak instead of trying to win her back?" She shook her head at this, and Leo, who had been carrying this thing inside him for far too long, let her see the truth, let her understand that it was exactly as she said, that he had fooled himself and been casually cruel to another innocent woman, one he still cared for, just because he thought that was the only way to forget about Nati.

"Come here, you foolish man," she said, opening her arms for a hug. Leo sank into it, burying his nose in her perfumed shoulder. It had been too long since anyone had offered him this simple comfort, and he realized how starved he was for it. "You see, if you had stayed in touch with me, I would not have let you make such a silly mistake." Tahira sighed, petting his hair and practically cooing. "Why not fight for Nati? Why did you just leave?"

He pulled back from where he was making a happy nest on her shoulder. "She told me she didn't love me anymore. That I wanted more out of the relationship than she did. I could have worked through anything, but not that."

"And you believed her?"

He spread his hands in confusion. "Why wouldn't I? Why would she lie to me?"

"Oh, dear," Tahira said. "You really are as daft as that wooden spoon. You have no Desi aunties in your life and it shows. What should I do with one like you?"

"But she said she didn't love me anymore," he repeated, like a child insisting on a point.

"Did you ever stop to ask yourself why a woman who was virtually inseparable from you for years, a woman who had taken you to meet her family, and invested so much time and energy in you, would turn around from one day to the next and tell you she never loved you? Just breaks up with you out of the blue, without any warning? Hmm, genius?"

"Stop, Tahira," Leo begged. A dizzying combination of nausea, horror and, at the very end of it, hope crawled its way up his chest.

"In your defense, Nati can be very convincing when she wants to be." Tahira adjusted the sleeves of her Missoni patterned dress, picking up the magenta hues of her headscarf, and Leo had to wonder briefly how she had the courage to wear that anywhere without fear of damage. It was that beautiful, as was everything she wore. "She is a chameleon, but she cannot hide her colors forever."

Leo pressed his fingers to his temples to relieve the mounting pressure. "Have you ever considered she might have actually meant what she said? That she didn't love me? Shouldn't I trust what the person I love says to me?"

Tahira beamed. "Person you love! That's wonderful. But no. You do not always trust what the person you love says to you, especially if there is a possibility that the person you love might be given to poorly thought-out acts of self-sacrifice." Tahira took Leo's hands, dropping her voice. "Talk to her. Please. Clear the air, tell her the truth without filter and try to discover what her truth is as well."

"I was planning to talk to her tonight." There was so much for him and Nati to get out in the open. "Are we good?" Leo asked, regret hanging heavy over him. He might not have made such a mess of his life if he'd only stayed close to the people who understood him. His mother and father cared for him, as did Genevieve—he knew this down to his bones. But staying in East Ward was no guarantee that he would have done better or worse; he simply wouldn't have been alone in his difficulties. This was his home and these were his people, and he'd compounded mistake upon mistake by leaving them behind.

"Depends on how good dinner is. I can vouch for my couscous, but not for anything else." The bell rang, startling them both.

"You're going to roll out of here by the time dinner is over. You'll see." Leo gave Tahira a quick forehead kiss. "Thank you."

"Be off with you. I will organize this mess," she said, shooing him before she turned to contemplate the catastrophe of his kitchen. Leo gave her a soft smile—things should have been this way. A house full of friends and food and love of every kind from the people who knew him best.

When Leo opened the door for Caleb and Nati, Caleb gave him a one-arm hug before showing him the contents of a ceramic dish through the plastic wrap. "Banana pudding, made fresh this morning," he said proudly.

"Still your dad's recipe?" Leo asked.

Caleb smile reached his sharp dark brown eyes. "You know it. Best banana pudding you'll ever taste."

Leo's mouth practically watered. Tahira wasn't the only one who would have to be carried out after tonight's meal. "One of my favorite desserts. Kitchen is back that way. Tahira's already here."

Caleb stepped past him, and Leo was able to put his full attention on Nati. Her gloriously curly hair hung loose and shiny. She wore a white V-neck T-shirt that looked very new and, despite its simplicity, very expensive. It was paired with low-riding slim-fit jeans, pink high-top Keds, and a matching belt. She looked like a college student instead of the medical professional that she was.

And her mouth. It looked as kissable as it had last night. He could still taste her on his lips.

Without a word, she pushed the cake container between them, practically under his nose. "Puerto Rican pineapple cake. Don't worry." She smiled, and it was like watching the sun rise inside his apartment. "I had nothing to do with making it. Val asked me to give this to you as thanks for bartending the other night."

Leo's eyes grew wide at the size and elegance of the cake, could smell the pineapple and vanilla, dense and aromatic, rising from the cake. He really wasn't going to make it out of dinner alive. "I told you—no more thanks."

"Go tell that to my sister. I stopped by to see her this morning, and she kept going on and on about how you saved the night, and how great you are. Guess you won her over again." Nati bit her lip at that last phrase, as if she hadn't mean to give that away.

"Come on," he said, taking her hand while balancing the cake in the other. He was tired of overthinking this. "I haven't finished setting the table. You can help me."

Nati allowed herself to be pulled behind him. Leo

watched with satisfaction as Tahira and Nati greeted each other, hugging and laughing as if they didn't see each other nearly every day. Caleb came to stand next to him, leaning into his side, picking at a small bunch of grapes.

"This is how it should be," Caleb said, popping another grape into his mouth.

Leo nodded, bopping Caleb on the forehead with a light rap of his knuckle. "It is. For the first time in forever, everything feels just the way it should be."

Caleb gave Leo a smile in response that was so bright, it forced his dimples deep into his cheeks. Nati, laughing at Tahira, sent Leo veiled looks that served as reminders of the moments they'd shared the night before. It was as close to perfect as Leo could have hoped for. The friends of his heart, all together in one place, with no doubts that they were exactly where they needed to be.

Chapter Thirteen

Nati

"Is it possible to die of overconsumption?" Caleb asked, rubbing his stomach.

"We die like heroes." Nati raised her glass of wine for emphasis. Leo and Nati's shared kiss, which they hadn't had a moment to talk about, hung unacknowledged between them, so prominently she was surprised Tahira and Caleb couldn't sense its echo even now that they sat around the table. But the awkwardness she'd expected didn't materialize.

Instead, she found Leo doting on her all evening. Though she was unaccustomed to anyone hovering over her like a mother hen, she didn't mind his attention. She didn't know what to make of it, but a part of her—actually, an enormous chunk of her—basked in it, and she thanked him often, which only made him grow bolder, willing to do more if only to hear her tell him how good he was, how very grateful she was.

When was the last time anyone had fretted over her in a way that didn't make her feel like an infant? She might not have needed Leo to pile on another helping of banana pudding or a second slice of pineapple cake, but she'd accepted it because it made her feel spoiled. This was something else she'd missed about being with him. He always managed to make her feel like she was worth all the attention he focused on her. For someone who wanted to avoid other people's fumbling attention, most specifically that of her family who too often still treated her like a baby girl, this was remarkable. Leo's attention didn't make her feel dimished.

The table had long since been cleared of everything except for desserts, which they continued to pick at despite being stuffed to the point of exploding.

"You are four-year-olds, each and every one of you," Tahira said, prim and put together as always, and at her perfect ease since she had not played the glutton like Nati, Caleb and Leo had. "You can have everything you want, but in the correct proportions." She raised a strong, elegant finger covered in tasteful gold rings. Balance is key to success in every field."

Leo glanced at her. "Still have acid reflux, don't you?"

Tahira tapped her lips with her forefinger. "That, too."

Nati giggled before leaning back in her chair. It was

like being back in school with them, except with better dishware and an actual dining room table, not eating off plastic picnic plates on foldable card tables. It's as if the years between the end of school and their current situation had never happened, and she felt those times as close to her as the warm breeze from the open window on her skin.

"So how did the review of the proposal go? Does it look good, boss?" Caleb asked, out of the clear blue.

"Caleb!" Nati said. "No shop talk. It's rule number one when we get together."

"What? I can ask. Leo doesn't have to answer. Right?"

Leo, who had been leaning in soporific bliss on his hand, blinked rapidly, apparently a half cake-slice away from falling asleep. "The clinic isn't my actual employment. Does it really count as shop talk?"

"It's shop talk, but you get a pass because dinner was incredible," Nati said, half-humorously, half-affectionately. He really had outdone itself, and her praise made him sit up a little straighter.

He eyed the last piece of cake on his plate as if it had offended him. "I don't want to raise expectations, but according to the rubric and everything that Nati showed me, you will most likely score very high, which gives you a good chance of winning the award. However—" Leo paused to let Caleb whoop and punch the air "—I am not the final judge. There might be other criteria that I am not aware of. Even with the rubric, the process is just subjective enough to be unpredictable."

Nati appreciated the sage way he answered—diplomatic Leo, as always. Tahira nodded to herself, which made Nati want to ask what was on her mind. She'd seemed odd the whole night, and Nati just hoped that she was okay. She reached a hand out to her, which Tahira took, squeezing gently.

"The opening night fundraiser went well. Better than I expected," Nati said.

Caleb snapped his fingers. "I was thinking we could partner with the local diagnostics laboratory and the outpatient radiology center to offer discounted services to patients we refer."

"I read about a clinic in Connecticut that does that. Still think we should have another portable ultrasound machine," Tahira said.

"That lab manager is a little obstinate." Nati sighed. "They're a franchise, and you know their primary goal is to make money. They're also the only lab service in that part of East Ward, so you can imagine how not inclined they are to give up any potential profit."

"Make a note of it, and we can discuss during our next meeting," Tahira said, glancing at her watch. "Caleb and I have a very early day tomorrow, so he agreed to take me home. We should get going."

"I…did…didn't I?" Caleb said, confused. God, they were so obvious. Nati exchanged a glance with Leo that told her he was thinking the exact same thing.

"I seem to recall you saying that as well," Leo said, visibly suppressing a smile.

"Okay, then," Caleb followed Tahira to her feet as well. "Thank you for dinner. My turn next time."

"You have a tough act to follow. Dinner was so very good," Tahira said, giving both Nati and Leo a kiss on the cheek. This, too, was familiar. Spending an entire evening with them, but at the end of the night, Nati and Leo were always left on their own.

"Call when you get in," Leo said as Tahira herded Caleb out of the apartment.

"Got it, boss!" Caleb answered just as the door closed behind him.

Nati stood in the foyer, the door shut before her, a handful of Leo's shoes scattered at her feet, while an assortment of jackets and coats seemed to have taken up permanent residency on their respective pegs. For the first time in a very long time, Nati didn't know what to do, relying on her sense of humor to get her through this moment. "They're cute even when they are trying not to be," Nati said.

She glanced at her bag and shoes, wondering if she should get going as well. But Leo put a hand on her arm, the touch radiating heat that sank in waves to her very bones.

"Don't go yet," Leo said, and it astounded Nati just how well he could read her. Even after all these years, she was still an open book to him.

"I know I have a big appetite, but even I don't know if I can eat any more," Nati quipped, reaching for a joke and watching her efforts fall flat. Leo hadn't let go of her arm, and the weight of it was beginning to spread to places she'd long neglected in favor of work and more work. All this just to dull the ache of not having this anymore, of not having this man, who made her question everything with just a brush of his hand on her skin.

"You don't have to eat. We can watch a little TV. Talk." He quickly averted his gaze, fixing his eyes on a point somewhere to the right of where Nati was standing before visibly forcing himself to look at her, an expectation within her growing louder with every passing moment he held onto her.

"We could…talk, I guess," she murmured, forgetting to call on her ability to mask her feelings, and no longer wanting to. There had always been something about Leo that made trying to hide from him impossible. All she could do was think about their kiss, how it had felt like finding something precious she'd lost, something she thought she might never have again. This was Leo, her first—possibly her only—love, and she was certain this was all a mistake, but it was a mistake she desperately wanted to make.

"I was actually thinking you should kiss me again," Nati said.

Leo dropped the hand that held Nati's arm. "I… didn't think—"

She stepped closer to him, the hand that had been on her arm becoming a hand on her waist, and she remembered this, too—his easy, expressive affection. It wasn't just sex appeal, though Leo had that in spades. He liked to touch and be touched, which suited Nati perfectly. It had been a long time since she'd touched anyone in a meaningful way, and she felt the gnawing hunger of her starved state. Nati had gone from hesitation and rationalization to pure need, a need that she was tired of denying herself.

The soft rasp of his short beard against her hand as she cupped his face had Nati reeling with the onslaught of both familiar and unfamiliar feelings. She leaned forward, leaving a chaste kiss on his lips that had them both shivering. It was always going to be like this, wasn't it? Every single time Nati kissed this man, she would experience this sizzling jolt of heat straight to her core that had her thoughts shutting down until there was nothing left but him.

Leo answered by kissing her back. His lips fused to hers as his hands dropped to her hips and pulled her against him. Nati opened eagerly beneath him and took in the taste of him, made it a part of herself. The way he swayed his hips to the rhythm of Nati's tongue sent Nati's thoughts into oblivion, until she was made of only instinct. He could ask absolutely anything of her at this moment, and she knew she would give it to him, no questions asked.

Their kiss deepened, and she felt him swell against her, his hardness a living, throbbing thing pressed against the most tender part of her body. Nati did not restrain the moan that contact provoked. A fierce tremor rocked her as memories rushed through her, all the moments they had spent together, the times he'd kissed her and held her. Nati missed that, missed the sensations, but, more importantly, missed him. Missed how he understood her body, his ability to pull pleasure from her, and her own unselfconscious eagerness to give it back to him in turn. She missed all the ways he knew how to love her.

She pressed harder into the kiss, into his hips, tasting him, toying with him, coaxing him to show her more, to give her more, to take her back to a time when this was something she could count on having whenever she wanted. A time when she did a better job of cultivating this, keeping it safe. A time before she had thrown it away, no matter how perfect her rationalizations were for the actions she'd taken.

Only when he'd broken off and pulled back did Nati realize that she had threaded her fingers into the hairs on the nape of his neck. Her body had moved of its own accord with a certainty Nati did not entirely feel. She looked at Leo, searching for reassurance, but his expression was as blown away as she felt.

"Do you have any other bright ideas, Dr. Navarro?" Leo said, his voice raspy and wrecked. "Because I am incapable of formulating a plan of action here."

Nati snorted. "Plans are overrated." So was pining and regret. "I just want to go with this for tonight. Are you okay with that?"

Leo frowned a bit at this. "I would never expect you to do anything you didn't want to do."

"Same here. I don't want you to feel like you have to do more than what you're ready to do." Nati nuzzled into his neck, her nose pressing into the juncture at the base of his throat. She was gratified to discover, based on his gasp of pleasure, that he was still sensitive there.

"I had no plan except to eat and run, but I can adapt." Nati laughed into his neck, which sent another tremor through him. She pulled back, having mercy on him. "Your sofa looks comfy. What are you watching these days?"

Leo pulled back as well, pausing for a few moments to steady himself before taking her hand and leading her to his living room. "I don't have a whole lot of time, but I've been following this one series. Very dramatic, full of gorgeous, sexy people committing crimes they seem to always get away with." He pulled up the program on his streaming channel. "If you'd like to watch an episode with me, I don't mind rewatching until you're caught up."

That was an understatement. Leo had once driven Nati to the brink of endurance with the number of times he could watch the same show over and over.

"Depends how many times you've watched it already," she asked, curling up against his side.

"Only two or three times."

"For you, it's like watching it for the first time, every time." She stifled a yawn as his arm came around her waist. Desire strummed low in her belly, but Nati was also perfectly content to sit here with him, pressed warm and sated against his body. "Go on. Play it."

"You look like you're about to fall asleep," Leo said.

Nati snuggled in closer to him. "I promise. I won't."

Chapter Fourteen

Leo

Nati did, in fact, fall asleep.

Leo had felt that surge of want at her kiss, electricity licking at the edges of his spine and the tips of his shoulders. He'd grown painfully hard, and even now, he hovered at the edge of desire that had him attuned to Nati's every physical shift. It was delirium inducing to have her lying against him, her heat enveloping him, after not having had her for so long. He wanted her desperately, but he also wanted this, to watch her for hours as her even breathing provided the backdrop to the quiet night.

"You're not watching the show," came Nati's voice from his side, startling him.

"I am," he lied, glancing quickly at the screen to see the familiar action unfolding.

"You're thinking so hard, I can hear you in my dreams." Nati lifted her head, her curls taking on a life of their own. "What's got your brain so busy?"

Leo lowered the volume on the TV, debating on an answer and deciding on honesty. "I was thinking of you. How good it feels to have you here."

Nati tilted her head, all soft browns and caramels staring up at him. He was sure she was going to tease him—Nati couldn't let the opportunity to tell a joke get away from her. Instead, she lifted her hand to his cheek, thumb running across his cheekbone, lingering soft as an exhale on his skin, arresting Leo with the delicate sensation.

"It feels good to be here." She smiled before pulling him down for a kiss, softer and sweeter than the one they'd shared earlier. When they pulled apart, Leo kissed a path along her jawline, ending just under her ear, the skin silky. He tugged at her earlobe before murmuring, "Stay with me."

It was Nati's turn to shiver. He'd been doing that a lot tonight. She nodded against his cheek, inhaling his scent without any effort to hide how deeply she took him in to her.

"Say it. I don't want any more doubts between us. We already have so many."

Nati hummed, low and husky and rippled through with want. "Yes. I'll stay tonight."

With ease, Leo pulled her onto his lap, her strong legs straddling him. Nati looked down at him from under a cascade of curls, eyes hooded with the kind of lust that had fireworks bursting in his head, lips primed for another hundred kisses from him. The image was laced with familiarity but also with the realization that Nati was here, with him. The world became suddenly new with endless possibilities. He thought of his conversation with Tahira, the need to clear things up with Nati.

But Nati was here, and he was hungry—ravenous, even—for her, and he didn't have the willpower to give this up.

Nati's skin had always been soft, hypersensitive to the gentlest touch. He caressed her that way now, the tips of his fingers shimmying up her T-shirt and dancing along the ridges of her spine, like tapping the keys of a saxophone, an instrument that he'd learned how to use when he was in elementary school. Her breathy moans emerged at husky intervals beneath the insistence of his touch, like a song he was playing on her skin.

He swallowed those sounds with kisses that emptied the air from both their lungs, leaving them panting. He swelled with arousal, which Nati felt, because she ground down on his erection with a precise and determined swirl of her hips.

"My *colibri*, what are you doing?" he whispered.

Nati went rigid before pulling back, as if she'd been slapped. Leo's dread rose hot and desperate in him. "Did I say something wrong?"

Nati shook her head vigorously, shivering on his lap. "Say it again."

"Mi colibri?" he asked.

"You said it the other night," Nati whispered. "I never thought I'd hear you call me that again."

"Last night. In the cab." Leo ran a hand over Nati's curls, careful not to snag any of those gorgeous golden ringlets. "I've always thought of you that way. First my hummingbird, then Nati."

"I like that." Nati's smile turned wicked, and she dropped her head to rain kisses on his neck and shoulders, alternating with bites that had him arching into her. She soothed his small wounds with her tongue, careful to leave them where he could cover them with clothes. But she wanted to mark up his fine skin, leave him with a reminder that she had been there for the time it took them to fade to small bruises.

She pulled the edge of his T-shirt aside, seeking greater access to his collarbones. Leo did her the courtesy of whipping it off and flinging it away.

"I like that shirt," he said by way of explanation.

"Far be it from me to ruin a shirt just for the sake of sexy times."

Leo's laughter broke out of him in waves. "You talk like you still live on Tumblr."

"Maybe I do," Nati answered. "Maybe I have a whole online personality. There's a lot about me that's new, things you don't know yet."

Leo loved that word, *yet*. "But I will. You'll allow me to learn how you've changed? This isn't a one-off, is it?"

Nati frowned at him. "Only if you'll let me learn you as well. Fair enough?"

He pulled her hips forward, grinding up into her core, which had the satisfying result of making her yelp aloud. "Fair enough."

He brought his hands forward to skim the edge of her breasts, down over her ribs, forcing more shivers and moans from her. Her stomach rolled and quivered each time he touched her. He was shaking with the urge to tear every shred of clothing from her and plunge into her, slide home after an eternity away, but he restrained himself. He hadn't spent years fantasizing about being with her for it to be anything less than good for her.

Leo kissed her once more before carefully removing her T-shirt. The pink bra underneath drew his attention to the pink belt and the pink Keds that sat next to the door and couldn't help the laughter that bubbled from him. "You matched your underwear to your high-tops?"

Nati followed his gaze. "I warned you. I have an expensive clothing habit."

Leo left a kiss on the sculpted sweep of her collarbone before hooking his finger on the strap of her bra and pulling it down, unclasping it with his other hand. "I'll be careful."

A hiss of pleasure was her only answer. She scraped her fingernails down the nape of his neck and over his back, against which he arched in response, the contact with Nati's naked breasts making him go cross-eyed with need. He cupped them, kneading their fullness in both his hands as he kissed her with a greed that had his heart echoing its explosive pace in his ears. They were still half dressed, and he was a stroke and a kiss away from an orgasm. That wouldn't do.

"Let's get these off," he said, and he maneuvered her onto her feet so she could shimmy out of her jeans and underwear. She hadn't changed in these six years, her body still a wonderful mix of muscular strength and curvy softness. He ran a palm over the swell of her abdomen, squeezed the soft curve of hips that flowed from a small waist rippling with muscle underneath. And her thick, solid thighs, firm and smooth, the soft down of trimmed hair that begged to be explored and kissed.

He looked up at Nati's blissed-out expression as he showered kisses along all the spaces his hands had traversed before hiking her leg over his shoulder and exploring her secret places, the sweet taste of her forcing him to undo the button and zipper of his own jeans from sheer discomfort. Nati sighed, then moaned, then wobbled as she steadied her hands on his shoulders, his tongue's exploration alternating with his fingers in a rhythm that had her undulating her hips in time with his movements.

"I'm close," she warned, and he prepared himself to catch her when she climaxed.

He followed her lead, watched the frantic rolling of her hips, the frenzy of her breathing that grew more furious, more intense, until finally she came apart in endless waves. Her knees gave out and soon she was straddling his lap again, shaking with aftershocks. Leo stroked and kissed and clung to her until she was thoroughly wrecked.

"Hmm…" was all she could manage. He was rock hard and aching, but he put his own arousal aside to savor a rare moment of surrender, Nati's pliant tenderness and undisguised need for care as she slowly recovered. When she turned her face to kiss him, she ground down on him, a signal that she was ready for more.

Careful not to dislodge her, he fished his wallet from his pants and pulled out one of the condoms he always kept there. With Nati's help, he tugged his pants and underwear down, ripped open the package. Nati slid the condom over his length, the heat of her fingers forcing a moan from him.

Nati kissed him the entire time, pressing his head against the back of the sofa as she lifted herself into position and sunk slowly down on him, making sure he felt every inch of her. They broke off, gasping, sharing each other's breath until he was fully sheathed inside of her.

"I'm so full," she half gasped, half moaned into his ear. Her words set off something in Leo and he gripped her hip and pushed up into her, slotting his remaining length with a force that sent ripples of energy through them. Nati bit into his shoulder as he held her head firmly in place, his hips surging with all the repressed desire he'd been holding onto since the day he left her, fueled by loneliness and heartbreak and the insatiable need for someone he could not reach. Each thrust of his hips, each grunt was a complaint she answered with a matching need of her own. Wordless and direct, each surge of her hips, each kiss, knit something that had come undone inside of him, a fear and a trauma that she was not erasing but overlaying with this new experience, with the bounty of this beautiful body and heart against his.

Nati cried out, bit him hard enough to bruise, taking control of the pace until sweat broke over her, her curls sticking to her skin. As close as he was to finishing, he held on for her, waiting, always waiting, until she came, head thrown back, the long column of her neck tense, then slack as she fell forward and finally, finally, after an interval of endless waves breaking over him, he surrendered and gave himself to her.

It wasn't his alarm that woke him after. The sound, melodic and piercing, invaded his sleep and stirred the golden warmth he held in his arms. Nati unwound herself from his hold and moved in the direction of the ringtone.

"Hey?" came Nati's groggy voice upon answering what Leo's still-sleeping brain came to register as her phone. He wondered briefly if she was on call, but her reaction—at first stiff, then shaky as she asked a series of questions in a voice very close to the one she used for work, except for the edge of something that sounded like fear.

"When did this happen?… Where are you now?… Okay, I'm on my way." Nati ended the call and put her head down on her folded knees, the duvet of Leo's bed pressed against her chest.

Leo sat up, suffused with worry. It was early, not even six o'clock based on the still-lit cell phone she'd tossed aside, though dawn was already making its appearance in grey light that snuck in between his bedroom blinds. *"¿Que pasó?"*

Nati lifted her head, her breath slow and measured, as if she were focusing on controlling her breathing in a very precise rhythm. "It's Papi. He's in the hospital. I have to go." She flung the duvet off, her body coming alive with purpose.

"I'll go with you. But first, why is Enrique in the hospital?"

Nati answered from the living room, where she had cast off her clothes the night before, in a voice that was not her own. "He went into work this morning and collapsed. He's in the ER now. I need to go to him."

"Nati," Leo said, throwing off his side of the duvet, heedless of the fact that they were carrying on this conversation completely naked. "Hold on. I'll come with you."

"You don't have to," she said, reentering the bedroom as she put on her clothes. "Where's your bathroom?"

He stood in front of her, arresting her movements. "Nati, stop for a moment. Catch your breath."

Nati tilted her head, pale-faced and thin-lipped. He was sure she was going to curse him for slowing her down, but she didn't. She let out a sigh and surprised him by wrapped her arms in an iron grip around his waist.

"I'm sorry. I'm just... I can't seem to move fast enough."

"I know something about that," he said into her hair, smoothing his hand down her back. "But you're not alone. Get cleaned up. I'll call a cab and we'll go to the hospital together."

"I don't want to bother you," she said into his chest, hot breath seeping into his skin. "You've had so much trouble already."

"You're not troubling me. Please." He pulled back to lift her chin. "I want to be here for you."

She nodded before unclasping her arms and stepping out of his embrace. "Thank you. That means a lot to me."

If only she knew what he was willing to do for her. He had lost so much when he'd left, but he found something he never thought he'd have again when he came to East Ward to be with his father. He wouldn't let this chance slip through his fingers again. But first things first. Nati needed to see her father. They could deal with everything else afterward.

Chapter Fifteen

Nati

Nati fidgeted with her phone, as if she wouldn't hear it if it rang in the stale air of the car. As if staring at it, mindlessly polishing it and clicking on the home screen every ten seconds would soften the news that her father had collapsed and was now in her emergency room, waiting to be admitted. On her free night, of all nights. She wasn't even on the team that would treat him. She'd spent ten years in medical school, training day and night to work in this ER, the same one her mother had been brought to before she passed, preparing for the moment her family would need her, just so she'd have the night off when that moment came.

She didn't blame herself for the loss of her mother.

She'd only been twelve years old. But she was old enough now, and she hadn't been there for her father when he needed her. The irony would almost be comical if the stakes weren't so high.

She glanced over at Leo, who stared out the front window, though on occasion, his eyes flickered to her face, and she knew he was watching and assessing.

"You didn't have to come. Not after everything." After that wonderful dinner and their amazing night. It felt like last night had happened to someone else.

"I wouldn't have left you alone in this," he said, taking her hand in his. "Not for anything in the world."

Nati looked down at the hand that rested on hers and threaded their fingers together. He was so warm and solid and hers for the moment. A possible delusion she was willing to indulge to not face that other, darker thing that waited for her in the hospital. The thing she could not—must not—imagine, because a world without her father was a world she didn't know how to live in.

"Thank you," she whispered. And then there was silence until they arrived at the familiar entrance of the hospital. She was out the door and at the reception desk before the car had even stopped moving. Leo joined her once he'd sorted out the fare.

"Vanessa," Nati said. "I'm here for Enrique Navarro."

The familiar receptionist's usually chipper face was full of compassion. It was a look she usually reserved for distraught families of patients who had been yanked out of their beds and into a nightmare. Now that look was directed at Nati; she had become a member of one of those families. "He's in ER room 12. Your brother and sister are already back there."

"Thank you." She and Leo headed toward Papi's room. There were limits to how many people could go into the patient area at the same time, but this was her hospital. Everyone knew her and her family. They'd bend a little for her.

"Dr. Reinhardt," Nati said, recognizing the doctor on call.

"Dr. Navarro," said the tiny woman with straight blond hair and sharp blue eyes, examined Papi's chart. She was a colleague of Nati's, a sometimes friend and someone Nati could trust to do good work. If someone else had to treat Papi, Nati was glad it was her. "Vasovagal syncope. Your father fainted from a sudden drop in pressure. He's on an IV treatment right now."

"Current medication?" Leo asked.

Dr. Reinhardt's gaze lingered on Leo, clearly struggling with the decision to answer, but Nati relieved her of the dilemma with a quick nod of her head. "He was switched to Ibesartan when his numbers came in too high."

"Meaning it could be exhaustion, or it could be the medication," Leo said, his mind visibly working.

"May I see his chart?" Nati asked.

"Sure," Dr. Reinhardt said, releasing Leo from her scrutiny and giving Nati a small smile. "I know it's scary, but if the tests come back like I suspect they will, all your father is going to need is an adjustment of his medication and a vacation."

"Maybe this time he'll listen," Nati said.

Dr. Reinhardt nodded before indicating Leo. "New doctor in the house?"

Leo visibly started, as if remembering himself. "Dr. Espinoza. I'm just visiting family, though. Thanks for—" He waved his hand to indicate himself and Nati, who looked up from reading Papi's chart to watch the exchange.

"Only because it's Nati's father and she's here with you. Otherwise, I run a pretty strict emergency room."

Leo dipped his head in acknowledgment. "Duly noted."

Dr. Reinhardt took the chart Nati handed back to her. "I'll get those lab results to you as soon as they're ready."

"Thanks, Vicky."

Dr. Reinhardt took another look into Enrique's room before heading off in the direction of the nurses' station.

"I'll stay out here so you can spend time with your family," Leo said when the doctor was out of earshot.

Nati slid a hand over his arm, squeezing his wrist. "If you want to go. I don't want to—"

"I'm not going anywhere," Leo said, and Nati didn't miss the way his words brooked no argument.

She nodded before stepping past Leo to see her father. Rafi, looking pale and unkempt, leaned against the hospital bed, watching his sleeping father, and Val, who looked like she'd gone through twelve rounds of sparring and more abuse than one of her lettered aprons at the end of a shift, stood on his other side.

"Nati," Val said upon seeing her sister and rounded the bed to give her a hug. "He's going to be okay."

Nati held her tight, inhaling her familiar aroma, the smell that always meant comfort and home. "I know. The doctor told me. Philip?"

Val gave her a weary smile. "Philip and Étienne went to get us some decent coffee. They'll be back soon."

Nati glanced over her sister's shoulder to observe her father lying quietly in the hospital bed. "Is he resting?"

"Yeah," Val whispered, pulling away. "It really took it out of him."

"I don't know why he thinks he has to do everything alone." Rafi's voice cut across the space, a low strain of anger curdling the edge of his words.

"It's not Papi's fault," Val said quietly. "I abandoned him. I put all this extra responsibility on him when I opened the new restaurant. I shouldn't have done that—"

"Don't you dare," Nati interrupted. "You did everything to make it easy for him to handle the restaurant while you opened the second one."

Rafi gave Nati a kiss in greeting before saying, "She's right, Val. He chose to overdo it. He chose not to respect what the doctor has been telling him for months."

"Val," Nati said, smoothing her hand over her sister's hair. "Dr. Reinhardt said he just needs a vacation, that's all."

"He's been tired for a while, Nati." Val's eyes welled with tears, which she rapidly blinked away. "He wouldn't have had to do any of that if I hadn't been so selfish—"

"Basta, mija," Papi's voice came from the bed. It was raspy on a good day; now it sounded positively wrecked. "Your brother and sister are right. I overdid it." He rubbed his face with the hand that wasn't strapped in with needles and an IV line. "It's Gabriela's way of telling me that I need to take things a little bit more slowly."

"Figures it would take a sign from Mami to get you to do the right thing," Rafi groused even as he smoothed back the curls that tumbled over his father's forehead.

"Are you going to cut your hours at Navarro's?" Nati asked. "Because I won't believe it until I see it."

"The restaurant is your mother's and my dream," he said, his voice growing firm. "I won't just abandon it because I'm getting old."

And there it was again. The wound at the heart of the Navarro family, the pain from which everything else flowed. The death of his wife, their mother, and the ripples that event had had on all their lives. Still had on their lives. Nati was gratified by how her family was moving forward, into the future, but in too many ways, they were still tied inexorably to the past.

"Nobody is telling you to abandon it," Nati said. "But there are ways to manage a restaurant without killing yourself."

"And what, spend the day on the steps, watching traffic pass? I can't do that," Papi said.

"Oh, I don't know, Papi. You could try to stay alive long enough so you can take care of your grandchild. *¿Que piensas de eso?*" Rafi exclaimed.

"Rafi," Val said softly. "It's okay."

"It's not okay," Rafi retorted. "He's just running himself into the ground because he's afraid of a little boredom? Now who's being selfish?"

"Rafi," Nati snapped before turning to her father.

"Dejalo," Papi said. "He's just upset. Right, *mijo*?"

Rafi snorted like an angry puppy.

"Papi, he's not wrong. You're too caught up in the past," Val said, approaching her father and placing a hand on his arm. "Mami would understand if you slowed down."

"Pero your Mami isn't here." His face fell, and soon the three of them circled his bed. "For her, I would have retired. Taken her on cruises, or gone back to Puerto Rico to visit our family." Papi twisted the sheet in his lap. "She left before we could do that."

"Ay, Papi," Rafi said, sighing deeply. "It's like you're punishing yourself because she's not around. She wouldn't have liked that kind of thinking."

"She belongs in the past, Papi, even if we feel her with us," Nati said quietly. "You have to figure out a way to live where you are now, no matter what came before."

Papi wiped a tear from his face. "I don't think I'll ever be ready to put her in the past."

There was nothing to say to that, and who was Nati, of all people, to argue with him? Nati, who'd just spent the night with her first love, the man she'd let go of but could never really let go of. Nati rested her head on Papi's shoulder while Val and Rafi each took his hand. Nati's heart broke for both her and her father.

"Nati?"

Nati lifted her head to see Leo at the doorway and felt a swell of happiness overtake her, even if it was tinged with the melancholy flavor of this moment. The way she'd felt back in medical school, seeing Leo after hours of studying or working and practically being carried away by her elation. There had been no stress, no disappointment that the day could bring that wasn't relieved by seeing Leo at the end of it.

"Leo," Val said, tapping Papi's hand. She came around the bed to greet him. "It's so nice to see you again."

Leo's appearance at the restaurant, after not having seen the Navarros for so many years, felt less weighted than this moment. Rafi, who never passed up a chance to tease his sisters, was somber, his entire attention fixed on Papi except for a brief acknowledgment when his eyes made contact with Leo's. Val was wiping tears from her cheek, and Papi simply watched, like he always did, taking in what was happening around him with that innate calm that only rarely cracked, as it had tonight.

"Thank you." Leo approached the bed. "Señor Navarro. *Todo bien*?"

"Better now," Papi said, his voice dry and cracked. "This must be a strange déjà vu for you."

Leo nodded. "I've had better memories. But you look good. It will be only be a matter of a few hours before you are discharged."

Nati handed Papi a cup with water from the tray near his bed. "Here. Drink this."

"Gracias." Papi took the cup and sipped it carefully

before handing it back. "*Y tu*, Leo? You have to tell me what you've been up to in California when I get out, *si*? I haven't seen you in a very long time."

"It has been a while," Leo said in that way he had of answering without actually sharing information.

"Nati, bring him by the restaurant, *si*?" Nati made to protest—there was no way Papi was planning on going back to work after this incident—but Papi raised his hand to stop her rant. "Don't worry. I will not serve him. I'll meet him as a customer, okay?"

Dr. Reinhardt poked her head into the room. "I'm sorry to interrupt. We just need to complete the discharge paperwork."

"I'll talk to her. Thanks, man," Rafi said to Leo before patting his father's arm and saying, "I'm bringing you home. I'll pick up some of your things later."

"No, *mijo*. I don't want to bother you," Papi said.

"Yeah, Rafi, I can stay with him," Nati interjected.

"Honey, you work too much, and he needs someone to keep an eye on him. I have sick leave. He'll stay with me," Rafi answered.

"It's only for a few days," Papi said, trying to sound stern and failing spectacularly.

"You'll stay for as long as the doctor suggests." Rafi nodded in Leo's direction before leaving the room. All of Rafi's overprotectiveness was thankfully directed toward his father, with none to spare for Leo.

"Leo, if you want to go, you can. I don't want to make you wait," Nati said.

Leo shook his head. "Are you sure? I don't mind."

"I know. But it might take a while. You know how these hospitals can be."

He laughed and Nati drank in the sound of it. "I do, as it happens." He ran a hand from her shoulder, down her arm to capture her hand and squeeze it. Only a few short weeks ago, she'd been railing internally about this man showing up in her life again and dragging behind him all the pain and heartbreak of those last days before he'd left. And now, she couldn't stand to be without his hands on her, steadying her and pleasing her all at once. She didn't want him to go, but her family needed her, and she couldn't forget that his family needed him as well.

"I'll check in on you," he said.

"Okay," she said, her lungs empty of air. God, she wanted to kiss him, not once, but over and over again. It was reckless and foolish to let herself slide back into the way she felt about Leo without being absolutely clear about what it all meant. Despite this, she wanted to be reckless and foolish again if it earned her even one more kiss.

But her father and her family were in the room, and Nati worked here, and for a million and one reasons unrelated to this moment, it was best to wait.

"Bye, Leo. And…thank you," She dipped her head and the mischief rose unbidden. "For everything."

He laughed again, shaking his head. "Nati, you are the messiest person I have ever met."

That's why you loved me. Once. "Yeah, I get that a lot."

Leo hesitated, his soft green eyes holding a promise that had Nati teetering on the edge of self-control. What was he offering her and why? Did he hope to forget his old life? Was he looking for the comfort of the familiar as he stood poised at the edge of possibility? Did these first steps toward a new life scare him so much that he sought to cling to the one person he knew better than anyone?

Nati didn't want to be his shield, his security blanket, his fortress. It meant he would leave as soon as he was strong enough. She wanted to hunker down behind the same walls he did, and be weak or strong with him. Not in front or behind but at his side. She'd abandoned him once, and God knows, she'd done it with only him in mind. But she would never do that to them again if given half the chance.

Whatever was in his eyes at that moment, she couldn't answer him. Not in view of her family. Those words were for another time.

Nati had gone home after discharge to pack a bag for her father, which Étienne picked up, while Val and Rafi got him settled in at Rafi's place. Nati was familiar with pushing herself in extremis, knew how to manage exhaustion, to harness energies that were nearly depleted in an effort to keep her going. But when she returned to her apartment, she was wiped out in ways she hadn't known she could be. Terror for her father, anguish for her siblings and a night spent with Leo that had not cured her uncertainties—her body was close to shutting down.

She threw herself on the sofa, which her cat, Loiza,

took as an invitation to jump on her chest and purr loudly.

"¿Hey, como estás, mi bebe?" Nati cooed, peace winding through her as Loiza's rumble echoed through her chest. She buried her nose in Loiza's white fur, inhaling the distinct scent of her spoiled little cat. Her mind kept returning to Leo and the way they'd said goodbye, how incomplete it had felt. He'd stayed for her and she was moved each time she thought of it. Before she could talk herself out of it, she pulled out her phone, opened Leo's contact and typed in a message.

Thanks again for today.

Nati stared at the phone before hitting send. She set the phone down, threading her fingers through Loiza's fur. She would thank Leo a thousand times if she could.

The vibration of her phone offered a counterpoint to Loiza's purr.

I would have stayed to the end if you'd let me.

Nati's hand froze, her breath coming hard and fast. Like everything else Leo said, intentional or not, the text was like a knife wound to the heart. She found herself in the blurred frame of past and present, unsure of where exactly she belonged. Her hands shook as she glanced at the clock. I'm just getting home.

This was a dangerous game she was playing. She didn't just want him on the phone—she wanted him here, next to her, giving her comfort that was as much physical as emotional. More than just a squeeze of the hand and a brush of lips. She wanted him to comfort her in every way, and she had no idea how to ask for that, if she should even hope for it.

How's Enrique?

Nati exhaled. This was better. At Rafi's. He'll be there for a few days.

That's a relief.

Nati twiddled her thumbs, wondering what else she could say. Dinner was good. You could give Val some competition.

She could imagine the smile that creased his face, how happy her comment probably made him. Leo loved praise, loved to be told that he'd done well. If it was so good, let's do it again.

She giggled. Such audacity. You don't waste time, do you?

A pause while he thought or typed. Loiza had circled her chest and settled into a position that was designed to make it harder for Nati to text. That cat was not in the mood to share her attention.

I've wasted enough time.

No, he hadn't. He said these words to her as if they were true, but his actions had shown something else.

He actually hadn't wasted a single moment, going from his supposed heartbreak over Nati to getting married not even six months later. She had half a mind to tell him that, but she wasn't in the mood for the inevitable denials. And of course, he would deny it—she'd ended things with him first, so who was she to be offended? And yet, she was. Deeply and profoundly offended. He'd married a woman once to get over her. How could she be so sure he wasn't doing the same thing to Nati, using her to get over his failed marriage?

Nati? Can I call you?

Nati shook her head as if he were in front of her. She knew she would have to translate that into an answer he could understand. That was the problem, wasn't it? She wanted him here, with her, despite everything that had happened. Her heart wasn't interested in her offenses or in remembering that she pushed him away and how he had eventually and so easily let her go. She wanted him here, not even to go back into the past, but to do something new, something different. Build something that might last.

Instead, she wrote I'm dozing thanks to you. Can I call later?

She tossed the phone next to her, ignoring the quick buzz of Leo's response. It had been a really hard day, and she wasn't in the mood for delusions—not his, and certainly not her own.

Chapter Sixteen

Leo

Leo did something he never did—he called Caleb to confirm that Nati would not be coming in to work for a few days. After her father's collapse, anything outside of asking after his health felt a bit tone-deaf. She texted him regularly with updates but had not alluded again to anything between them. He decided he should wait for a sign from her that he could approach, give her time to work out her own family situation. After all, he had some recent experience in the field on the patient side.

Instead, he arranged to stop by and visit Enrique. Étienne greeted him at the door, all tall grace and charm.

"Leo! You found us. Come, come." Étienne stepped aside, allowing him to enter. "Beautiful spring weather, eh?"

"Good weather for a bike ride," Leo said, handing off a fruit platter he'd picked up on the way.

"Is that your hobby?" Étienne asked, and Leo felt his genuine interest.

Leo nodded. "I've been cycling for years. One of the advantages of living in California—there are a lot of trails."

"I like this," Étienne said, indicating with outstretched hand the living room. "May I offer you something?"

Leo shook his head. "Don't trouble yourself. I just wanted to check in with Enrique and see how he was doing."

"I'll let him know you're here." Étienne stepped past him down a corridor that Leo guessed led to the bedrooms.

Leo took in the apartment—colorful, lived in, rich with texture and light shown to best effect with a golden spring afternoon shining outside the window. His sister's apartment was a bookish den, soft and cozy and just this side of too cluttered. Rafi and Étienne's apartment was a vibrant cacophony of busy colors that contained a thread of unexpected order, which Leo suspected best reflected the style of the couple who lived there. Étienne was a successful photographer, evidenced by the extraordinary art on display.

"Leo." Rafi's voice drew him away from his contemplation of one of the many photographs on the wall.

Unlike Étienne, Rafi held himself a little bit aloof. Justifiable—he had no idea what Leo's intentions were and he had the stress of a sick parent, a stress Leo understood only too well.

"I'll take you back." Rafi tried for a smile that looked more like a grimace. Leo felt a little sorry for him.

"Hey," he said, pausing in the hallway before they reached Enrique's room. "Your father's collapse must have been really scary for you. But as a medical professional, I can say with confidence that your father will be up and around in no time."

Rafi bit his lip, a frown marring his otherwise smooth face. "Yeah, I know. I just didn't need the reminder of his mortality just yet, you know? I'm still a little freaked out." Rafi considered him. "But I guess if anyone gets it, it would be you. How's your dad?"

"Better," Leo said. "You hear cancer, especially the kind he has, and you automatically think the worst. But he's progressing through chemo, and we're optimistic he'll get it under control."

Rafi smiled, a less brittle one than earlier. "These guys don't think twice about scaring the hell out of us."

"Nope. It's payback for all the times we scared the hell out of them growing up."

Rafi's face broke into a small laugh that made him less tense. Leo liked to think he might have had something to do with that. "Come on. Papi's waiting."

Upon entering the room, Enrique was sitting up in a large bed surrounded by pillows, the television playing on low across from him. When he saw Leo, he sat up straighter. Unlike Leo's father, who was still weak but getting stronger each day, Enrique looked like he was lounging in bed before getting up to confront the day.

"Hola, Senor. Lo veo bien," Leo said by way of greeting.

"That's because I am," Enrique answered, a gleam in his eye that reminded him of Nati. "Rafi won't let me out of bed."

"Doctor said three days of bed rest at least," Rafi said.

"That's what you say. I didn't hear that," Enrique said. Leo was surprised that the elegant, serene man he'd always known sounded like a petulant teenager at the moment.

"Maybe because you were unconscious?" Rafi retorted.

"What do you think, Leo? Doesn't three days sound like a lot?

Leo chuckled. "If it feels like a lot, it's because you're getting better. But if you do too much too soon, it will set you back."

"Thank you," Rafi said. "I swear, he's training me for fatherhood. He just doesn't realize it."

"Okay, okay," Enrique said, putting up his hands as if to ward off any more attacks. "I'll behave. Come sit here, Leo." He patted the edge of the mattress. "Rafi, why don't you get us some coffee, *por favor*?"

Leo was going to protest, but Enrique gave a quick shake of his head, and Leo clamped his mouth shut.

"You get decaf, okay? Doctor said to lay off the caffeine."

"Of course," Enrique said, a glimmer of something

flickering in his eyes. Leo nodded. This guy was up to something.

When Rafi left, Leo said, "You're going to try and drink mine, aren't you?"

Enrique laughed, nodding almost to himself. "Who can live without coffee? It's not normal."

Leo laughed. "I'm starting to think you are not the easy patient I thought you were."

"My children worry too much."

"You gave them a good reason."

"Maybe." Enrique nodded. "And your father? Is he better?"

Leo adjusted himself so he could better face Enrique. "Much, thank you."

"I'm happy to hear that. I used to see your father around East Ward. Very nice man." Enrique paused, observing Leo. "Nati was here last night. Slept right next to me. The others don't do that."

Tenderness welled up in Leo. He could envision Nati, so tough and independent, curling up next to her father like a little girl while her father slept. "She can be very sweet."

"She's the youngest," Enrique answered. "They are always babies, even if they want you to think otherwise. Especially her. Val tried her best to nurture her." Enrique shook his head. "We all tried."

Leo knew he was referring to the way Val had taken over the care of her siblings, tried to raise them while still being a teenager and taking over the restaurant. "I'm sure everyone did their best."

"Si, si," he said. "We all did. But it left a sign on all

of us. Gabriela was a force of nature. Losing her was like losing the anchor of this family."

Leo felt like Enrique was trying to convey something to him. He rolled the older man's words around in his head, trying to decipher his real meaning. "I'm sorry about the loss of your wife."

Enrique shrugged. "Nothing to do for it now. The kids are building their own lives. Everyone is moving on." Enrique leaned forward. "But if you understand what a big gap my wife left behind, you will have the key to understanding Nati. You get what I'm saying?"

Leo nodded. "I think so."

"Good. Oh, and also, buy Loiza treats before you go to Nati's house the first time. Your life will go much easier for you."

Leo just stared at Enrique. Was he giving him… love advice? Really? "I'll keep that in mind."

"Good." Footsteps in the hallway indicated that Rafi was coming. Enrique dropped his voice to a whisper. "Now, be good. I like my coffee sweet with sugar, okay?"

The doctor in Leo wanted to protest, warn Enrique away from this decision and encourage him to respect his doctor's wishes. But the lovesick Leo, the one who wanted at all costs to have Nati and figure out a way to keep her? The one who was hungry for any wisdom that might allow him to do this? That Leo had other ideas.

"Two sugars or three?" Leo answered.

Leo's resolution to wait until Nati reached out to him and asked to see him crumbled right after his visit with Enrique. After two days of not seeing her, he was back on his bad decision-making habit and decided to board the train directly from Rafi's apartment to Nati's. He made only one stop to pick up a pouch of cat treats, fish flavored, since he imagined all cats like fish.

Navarro's was open—Val had been right about setting up the restaurant to practically run itself to give relief to her father. He stopped in, expecting to see Val, but none of the Navarros were on hand. He ordered coffee and a bacon, egg and cheese bagel—a breakfast Nati had always been fond of—and found himself standing at the residential entrance of Nati's building, texting her from outside and being buzzed in.

Nati was still in a pair of flower-print pajamas, curls tied up in a scarf. Her pajama top had been poorly buttoned, showing a hint of flat stomach each time she moved, which had Leo repressing the urge to pant. "I wish you had warned me. I would have put on something less…" She swept a hand over her appearance as if it was explanation enough.

"It's impossible for you to look bad," Leo said, stepping inside her apartment. He pulled out his two purchases.

Nati gave him one of those sly looks that made him want to bay at the moon. "It must be true if you say so. What do you have there?" she asked, looking at his bag with interest.

"I bring gifts," he said cheerfully, showing her the bag with her breakfast sandwich inside and the cup of coffee that he'd done up himself—this time black with one spoon of sugar.

She half squealed in delight as she fished the sandwich out, holding it to her nose. "I was about to have cereal."

"You live above a restaurant," he teased, handing her the coffee cup as well before closing the door behind him. "Why would you ever eat a cold breakfast in your life?"

Nati shook her head. "Fair point. But that would require me to actually get dressed, and today, I was planning on putting that off for as long as possible."

A small meow drew his attention to a lovely tabby threading her way through Nati's legs.

"May I?" Leo asked, indicating the bag of treats.

Nati nodded. "Oh, Loiza will love you forever."

"Kind of the point," Leo said, unzipping the pouch and placing a few of the treats in front of Loiza. To his satisfaction, she nibbled them up, a low purr rising from the ball of fluff.

When Leo straightened, he took in the tired eyes, and pinched paleness of Nati's face. "I know it's been rough. I stopped by to see your father before coming here. He's ready to come home."

Nati raised an eyebrow. "Oh, trust me. I know he is. Meanwhile, I've been over there most days to keep an eye on him. But he's driving all of us to extremes by complaining the entire time."

"As you age, you lose the ability to just be anywhere. You yearn for the comfort of your own home, your own bed."

"Mmm," she said, stepping over Loiza and leading Leo to the kitchen where she set down the bag. "Coffee?"

"Bought myself one. I'm good."

Nati took a long drag from hers, humming in delight before sitting down and unwrapping the sandwich. "Good to know it will be a while till I yearn for the comfort of only my bed."

Leo laughed, taking the seat across from her. Why had he brought up beds? Nati had clearly rolled out of one after possibly losing staying with her father. She'd shared Leo's bed for only a few hours. All he'd been imagining since their first night together was the multitude of ways he could reacquaint himself with her body again. When they'd been younger and new to love, they hadn't been able to keep their hands off each other, and he felt the same way now. Even thinking about it made him physically uncomfortable.

But his desire went cold with the pernicious reminder that she had left him, a thought that had been tormenting him these last few days without her. His greatest fear—that he was setting himself up for failure in trying to repeat history—came roaring through him. He didn't think he could take another disappointment if she decided that he was still not the one for her.

"Papi is showing his age in that respect. But thank you," she said, suddenly so shy, he hardly recognized her. "I appreciate you going to see him. I know it means a lot to him. To us." She dropped her eyes to her hands, which were crossed in front of her. "You didn't have to."

"Enrique has always been good to me," Leo said quietly. "In fact, your whole family has always been welcoming to me. You would think, after what happened between us, they would have been colder, but no. Even Rafi was polite."

"Why would they treat you badly? You didn't cheat on me. You didn't lie to me. You didn't mistreat me. You were good to me when we were together, and they knew that I had never been happier than when I was with you." Nati frowned as she bit off that last part, and Leo leaned closer, awash in anticipation. They were on the edge of something, and he didn't want to rush past this moment.

"Then why?" Leo asked, his voice suddenly hoarse and cracked. "Why did it have to come to an end?"

Nati looked up, her vision clear and bright, too bright to be careless. "How else could it have gone? You had to take that residency, and I was too poor, too busy, too—"

"—scared?" he suggested.

Nati took a deep breath as if to steady herself. "Scared, but not of you or me. Never of what we had between us." She closed her eyes tightly as if holding something back before opening them again. "I was scared that you would have regrets and I would be the reason for those regrets. And I never wanted you to have a reason to say you were sorry for a choice you made. I never wanted to be the reason for you wishing you'd done something that you hadn't."

Leo got up from the chair he'd taken across from her and took the one adjacent to her instead, so he could hold her hand. "I wouldn't have regretted turning down that residency. Yes, it was prestigious and a great honor, and I've gotten so much out of it. Anyone would be envious of my job. But it was so far away from you, from my family, my friends." Leo kissed her hands. "If I knew then what I know now, I would have never let you get away from me."

"You had to go! It was too precious of an opportunity," Nati insisted. "And I wasn't going to be the one to hold you back, no matter what I was feeling at the time." She stared down at her feet, clad in the most ridiculous fluffy cat slippers he'd ever seen, and they looked perfect on her. "I wasn't worth giving that up for."

"Nati, I would have stayed. I would have traveled. I would have done anything."

"That's the problem, isn't it? You were willing to do anything and I couldn't… I wasn't going to let you do that." She looked up, her eyes flashing with something bottomless, something he recognized as grief. "No matter what it cost me."

He thought back to his conversation with Tahira and came to a slow, horrific realization. "Please don't tell me you broke up with me for my own good. Please tell me you didn't inflict all that pain and heartbreak because you decided that a job was more important than us."

"Not just any job. It was your career. Your life! It was important," Nati exclaimed, her voice climbing.

"To you! Maybe your career matters that much to you, more maybe than anything else. But it was never the case for me. You didn't have the right to project that priority onto me and make such a monumental decision alone without consulting both of us."

"Yes, I did!" she shouted, and Leo was blown back a moment by the force of her words. "Yes, I did, because you were ready to throw it all away. You were about to make the worst decision of your life if I didn't stop you. I was not going to let you say no to that opportunity. I was getting my dream residency. How could I let you throw away yours?"

Leo stood from his chair, pacing the kitchen in frustration. "It was my decision to make, not yours, Nati."

Nati moved as well, halting his pacing by standing right in front of him. "Tell me it was such a big mistake. Tell me you regret working for a world-class research hospital, one of the top ones in the world. Tell me I was wrong."

"I don't regret taking my job. How could I? But you made a unilateral decision about our relationship, and you have the nerve to justify it by telling me that because the job was so great, I shouldn't have regrets. But I do, Nati. I do. I regret not having been with you all this time." He couldn't believe she was being so obstinate about this. "We could have tried something. We weren't the first or last couple to be separated by distance."

Nati threw up her hands in frustration. "But that wasn't your first instinct, was it? Your instinct was to give up the chance and stay here instead. And if we had tried to make it work, what kind of relationship would that have been? Texting each other between eighteen-hour shifts? Spending money I, at least, didn't have, just to see you a few times a year? How were we supposed to pull that off?"

Leo pointed at himself, then at her. "That should have been our choice to make. Not yours. You didn't give me a chance. Didn't give us a chance. You just decided that things were impossible, and you did whatever you had to do without thinking what the effect might have been on me. That's very disrespectful position to take toward someone you're supposed to love."

Nati let out a dry, humorless laugh. "Oh, please, Leo! You got married six months after our breakup, and now you want to play the victim? What kind of effect did it really have on you?"

Leo glared at her. "You think I got married because I didn't care about you anymore? That I was over you? News flash—the worst mistake I ever made was to let you end things with me. The second mistake was to marry Michelle, hoping I could forget you." Nati made to protest but he put his hand up. "I know it was a jerk move, and I will always owe her something in this life for willfully making both of us unhappy. I get it. But I married because I thought it would get you out of my head. My heart. You can see how that worked out for me."

"Leo," she said with a voice laced with emotion.

"Don't." He didn't want pity from her. He wanted love. Commitment. Mutual respect. He wanted to know that she was just as desperate to be with him as he was to be with her. And he was afraid she was nowhere near a place to offer that to him. "I don't need you to feel sorry for me. I don't need you to buffer me from the consequences of my own decisions. What I need, what I've always needed, is to be with you as your equal, not someone you have to make decisions for because you think I'm too stupid or clueless to make my own. You were wrong, and the first thing you need to do is admit that."

"I have never thought that you were too stupid to make your own decisions."

"Haven't you? Why else would you take away my right to decide what to do with my life, with respect to our relationship, which theoretically should require both our input?"

Nati turned away, all pretense of calm evaporating. "Why are we arguing about this? We were younger and in a more difficult place. That's not who we are anymore."

"Throwing everything over our shoulder and telling me it's all in the past is not the approach, Nati. We need to talk this out and understand what went wrong. It's not all in the past. It's right here, in front of us. I want you to care. I want this to matter to you the way it mattered to me. I want it to mean more than anything else ever meant to you because if it doesn't, then there is no reason for me to be here. The time I'm spending on you is time I'm not spending anywhere else." He let the implication of those words sink in before stepping closer to her again, the world a sudden low hum in the background of his thoughts.

Nati was as she never was—speechless, without even a joke or a quip to ease this moment. Of course, she'd have nothing to say. He needed so little from her—an acknowledgment that maybe she'd made an egregious miscalculation and both of them had paid the price. But her resistance cooled his hopes. Why did he think this time would be different? Because she'd slept with him? Hadn't they slept together countless times before she cut him off? She might have rationalized that ending things was for his own good, but it had still been so easy for her to end things.

It was time to stop doing this. To stop setting himself up for disappointment. "I'm going to go. I was just checking on you."

"Leo, wait—" But just like then, her protest felt very half-hearted, like she was doing it for the formality of it, as if to say *yes, I tried to stop him, but he left anyway.*

It didn't matter. Leo had said more than enough. His family, at least, was waiting for him. And when that reached a state of equilibrium, he would go home to California.

He opened the door without looking back and left.

Chapter Seventeen

Nati

That had not gone well. Not one bit.

Nati could have stopped him, could have dragged him back inside her apartment and spoken to him, but she wasn't sure how to say what she needed to say. This was the conversation they'd needed to have ever since he'd come back to East Ward. And even knowing that this day would come and that she would be called to accounts for what had happened between them, she was still caught off guard.

She thought she was doing the right thing because she loved him too much to see him lose out. Not after all the sacrifices they had made to earn their degrees and secure their residencies. Not when getting a medical degree had been the single most important goal in Nati's life and she couldn't imagine anyone getting in the way of that for either of them.

But maybe she had miscalculated. It had mattered to her, more than anything else; at the time, it would have mattered more than Leo. But to Leo, nothing, not even his residency, had mattered more than her. And she'd taken away his chance to act on that. Even if she was still convinced it had been for his own good.

Her doorbell rang again, and Nati flew lightning-quick to answer it, thinking Leo might have changed his mind and come back after taking a few moments to cool off. But when she opened her door, it was Olivia instead. She couldn't rein in the disappointment as she stepped aside to let her cousin in. Olivia shoved a bakery box into her hands as she passed.

"Please, don't act so happy to see me," Olivia said, tossing her bag on a hook.

"I'm sorry. Leo was here and…" Nati threw her hands up in the air before losing herself in a whirlwind recollection of the morning. Olivia's voice pulled her back from her overthinking.

"Leo? Here? Did he wake up here?"

Nati gave her a withering look. "No, not this time," Nati said, rubbing her temples.

"What do you mean, not this time?"

Nati blinked as if coming awake. "I didn't mean… Well I did mean… Oh, for fudge sake, Olivia, I'm having a moment, okay?"

"About sleeping with him?"

"What? No, sex is always the easy part. I'm having

a moment because he's angry at me." Nati gave her the rundown of the conversation.

Olivia listened, quip free for once, which was strange and amazing at the same time. When Nati was done, Olivia thought for a few more moments before saying, "Nati, when is the last time you've admitted you made a mistake? About anything?"

Nati shrugged. "Forever, since I don't usually make mistakes."

"Hmm…" Olivia rubbed her chin, still thoughtful. "Do you think maybe this might be an exception?"

Nati pulled a face. "You mean this weird feeling is me feeling…sorry? I don't think so."

Olivia rolled her eyes. "How is someone who makes a living out of taking care of everyone else so completely sidelined by her own emotions? Not big on self-awareness, are you?"

Nati very nearly growled at her but found herself sinking into a chair. "How did I mess up so monumentally, Olivia?"

"Oh, well that's easy. You have to put yourself in another person's point of view for once. Tell me, when you broke up with Leo all those years ago, who were you really thinking of? Him or you?"

"Him! Of course, I was thinking of him," Nati said, trying to get the pounding in her head to die down.

"Guess again."

"Olivia…" Nati warned.

"Don't get snotty with me. If you had been thinking of him, you would have talked to him. You would have included him in your thinking. Especially given the fact that your decision impacted his entire life. No, little bunny, you were thinking of yourself."

Nati's stomach twisted. She hadn't wanted to admit it, but she had long since come to this conclusion. *She* had done this to them. Not Leo. This was all Nati's doing. She had built and destroyed by her very own hands. She just didn't want her cousin pointing this out because it made her feel exposed. Transparent. "Why do I feel like you're projecting?"

"I am projecting!" Olivia retorted. "I am one hundred percent projecting. Aleysha did the exact same thing to me. I recognize what's happening because I've been through it. If she had had even one-tenth the faith in me that I had in her, she would have talked to me about what was happening. She would have let me work with her. Instead, she thought she was being cute and noble by breaking things off. That's not loving someone. That's patronizing them. If you love someone, really love them, you take them into account."

"I do love him," Nati said quietly, the sense of nausea rising up in her. "I never stopped. I just thought, if I really loved him, I should be willing to sacrifice anything for him to be happy."

"And did it work? Was he suddenly happier after all that?"

Nati pressed her heel of her hands into her eye sockets. "To hear him say it, no."

"To hear him say it? As if he isn't the expert on his own feelings. Come on, Nati, you can do better than that."

"I need to talk to him."

"Yeah, you do. And I would appreciate some compensation for the free therapy."

"No, I don't owe you. You were just in here, crying about Aleysha the other day. And anyway, if you are so convinced about Leo, why don't you pick up the phone and call Aleysha? Why are you letting her control everything?"

Olivia opened and closed her mouth in quick succession. She clearly hadn't expected the salvo, and Nati experienced a flush of satisfaction, even though her cousin had only been trying to help her. Why should Nati be the only one to suffer? Even if Olivia was one hundred and fifty percent correct?

"Let's make a deal. You fix your mess with Leo, and I'll give my mess with Aleysha a shot."

"That's a lot of pressure for me to get things right."

"Your whole thing is working under pressure. If you can handle a ten-car pileup on the bridge, you can do this. Remember," Olivia leaned in. "The fate of all our happiness lies in your hands."

Nati had to physically restrain herself from biting her cousin. But she was right. Not about Olivia's situation—joke or no joke, her business with Aleysha was not connected to Nati and Leo. But Nati's happiness depended on Leo, and from what she'd learned today, his depended on her. And she'd played fast and hard with it because she thought she knew better than everyone. It would be up to her to fix it. They weren't going to survive another six years of pining and mourning mistakes.

Chapter Eighteen

Leo

Leo ignored his phone. It was never the person he most wanted to hear from. He didn't have the energy to pretend he was okay.

Tahira had tried to tell him during dinner what Nati had attempted to accomplish all those years ago, but it still stung. It was something his mother might have pulled—treating him like he was incapable of making any decent decisions of his own. His mother would have maneuvered and positioned and, yes, even manipulated him to get to the end she wanted.

He didn't need that from Nati, too. He needed to be able to trust the people around him; he didn't need someone who thought so little of him that they would choose to hoodwink him into making decisions instead of trusting him to make the right ones on his own. He and Nati could have tried to make it work, and she should have talked to him instead of ending things so decisively.

Leo considered his bar, wondering what he could make that might cheer him up, but he knew there was not one thing he could eat or drink that would take this bitterness out of his chest.

His phone buzzed loudly on the counter. Leo scooped it up, groaned at the notification that his mother was calling and sucked it up. This day wasn't going to get any better if he ignored her.

"Ma," he said, wedging the phone between his shoulder and his ear. He took out the ingredients he would need to make an old fashioned, the right combination of sharp and sweet that he would enjoy.

"Leo. Your father asked me to call you. Will you be stopping by today?"

Leo paused in his preparations, the jigger he held suspended in air. "It will be later this afternoon. I have to get in touch with the medical center and make arrangements to go back."

"So soon?" she said, sounding genuinely surprised. It grated on Leo.

"You seemed so invested in telling me how prestigious UCLA Medical is, how grateful I should be about working there. I have to go back at some point if I'm going to continue to be there."

"Aren't you?" she asked. "Grateful?"

"Yes!" Leo nearly shouted. "It's amazing. The best

job anyone could have. Short of being head of the research division, or chair of the board of directors, I can't imagine anything more prestigious. And it's the last place I want to be."

Her gasp was almost physical. "How can you say that, Leo? You should be honored to have that position. Your father and I would have done anything to have a job like that."

"Papá? Or you?" Leo retorted.

"What does that mean?"

All the anger and frustration of the last few hours burst out of him in a rush. "I am tired of everyone telling me what I need to do with my life. I am fully aware that my job is amazing, that it is possibly one of the best things that has ever happened to me. It's also true that I miss my family, and I would love to come home someday without having to feel like a heel for not putting my career first."

"This is about Nati, isn't it? This is her doing. She's convinced you—"

"Enough!" Leo slammed the glass he was holding on the counter, marginally aware that if it had been any thinner, he'd have to clean up a mess of shattered glass. "I need you to stop demonizing her. I don't know what your problem is, but you need to stop."

"She only cares about herself and her career. You were so quick to give up your residency to stay with her. Why was it never her who was willing to go be with you?"

"Why should she have done that? Her of all people, who had to fight so much to get what she wanted? In fact, why should any of us have had to give up anything? I know for a fact you wouldn't have."

"It's not the same," she said.

"Isn't it?" Leo let out a deep breath, trying to get control over himself again. "I need you to figure out why you have it out for Nati, but I need you to do it on your own time. I have to figure my stuff out on my own."

"Leopoldo Salvador Espinoza!"

Leo groaned. Not with the full name.

"Zoraida Quiroga Espinoza," he clapped back. He uncapped a bottle of gin, almost ready to chug it directly from the bottle. "Now, let me go. I have an appointment."

The last thing he heard was a huff of frustration before he ended the call.

He ran a hand over his face, scrubbing at his beard. A drink was looking less and less appetizing. Maybe a bath would be a better bet. He needed to center himself before he started to make the necessary arrangement to return to California. He wasn't sure what he'd do once he got there, but he needed to at least stay employed until he decided.

A ringing cut across the room, and he was poised to ignore it, except it wasn't his phone. He'd only had Caleb, Tahira and Nati as visitors since staying with his sister, so it took him a moment to realize that what he was hearing was the doorbell. He strode over to the screen on the electronic panel near the front door. He had to look twice to understand that he was seeing Nati, and that she was holding something in her hand.

He was almost of a mind to ignore the door and pretend he wasn't home, and he even paced to his phone to see that he'd missed two messages from her indicating she was on her way.

He wasn't sure what made him do it—hope, which refused to the die the slow, painful death that it should? Or maybe he just enjoyed suffering. Or maybe, just maybe, he saw a chance to say a few final things before putting an end to this last great milestone in his life.

He pushed the buzzer, indicating that she could come up.

When she knocked, he took a deep breath and opened the door. His heart was somewhere in his stomach, but he called on all his equanimity to speak to her. No surgery had ever made him feel this unsure of himself.

"Can I come in?" Nati asked.

"Yeah, of course." He stepped aside, allowing himself to look at her, note all her imperfections, try to gather to himself all the reasons why living without her wouldn't be so bad after all.

But it was an exercise in futility. Even with the lines of exhaustion on her face, the tired eyes, the frown that made her look heartbreakingly sad, she was always going to be the most beautiful woman he'd ever known. And what was more, she would always own his heart, and he was going to have to learn to live with that fact as well.

She stepped inside, waited for him to close the door and, without a word, offered him what looked like a shoebox-sized fabric box.

"You said that someone who could break up with you the way I did couldn't have cared much for you," she said without preamble.

Leo swallowed, the sound broadcast loudly across the empty space between them.

"Open it," she said.

Leo pulled off the lid and looked inside. "What are these?"

Nati pulled out a small notepad with stones and crystals hot-glued onto the cover. Gilded edges. Fountain pen with the name Natalía Navarro engraved on the side. "You gave this to me when I told you how much I love collecting pretty notebooks, even though I hate my handwriting."

He handled the notebook with care, remembering when he saw it in a small used bookstore and knew he had to buy it for Nati, for no other reason than because he knew she would like it. He couldn't speak; he was too caught up in the memories of those days, the way Nati was always at one remove from his thoughts, no matter what else was on his mind.

"And this?" She took out a bundle of cards and notes tied with a ribbon, like a stash of old love letters from a chest hidden in some attic. "These are all the birthday and holiday cards you ever gave me. I even kept the notes we passed during pediatrics. Do you remember? You were a pervert, by the way."

Leo couldn't help but laugh. Thank God their professor never caught them or, if he'd seen the notes, didn't care, given the amount of students in each class. That had been in their second year of school, and Leo remembered being particularly thirsty for Nati in that period.

"And this necklace? Do you remember giving it to me on New Year's Eve the third year we were together?" Nati pulled out the gold necklace with the pearl and diamond inlay. She had been so mad at him for spending all that money on her when she could never have reciprocated. But he'd put it on her and they'd waited until the fireworks were over, danced half the night away, and, on the first morning of the first day of the year, he'd made love to her while she wore that necklace, promising her that they would do this for every year they were together, for what he hoped would be the rest of their lives.

Nati waited as he held the necklace, dangling like captured starlight, glittering with the reflection of the sun through the window. Or maybe it was the flicker of tears that glittered on his lashes as every single memory spiraled out from this one, like a prism of light and color containing fragments of the moments they'd lived.

"You owe me six New Year's mornings," he said finally.

He'd only ever seen Nati cry once when they were working with senior doctors as part of their practicum team, and they had lost a patient. She'd felt like an utter failure and ached for the family who would have to mourn the young man. Now her face was wet with tears. "I know I do. And I will work as hard as possible to make those days up. You know I'm good for them."

"I do," he answered. "But Nati—"

"No, you listen to me. I had to fight so hard to get through school. My family, my *entire* family, made sacrifices so I could become a doctor. That's not me trying to earn your pity," she rushed to add when he made to protest. "It's just that, from where I was coming from, giving up any chance to further a career would have been inconceivable to me, because it wasn't just my sacrifice I was throwing away, but the sacrifices of everyone who had my back. I didn't become a doctor alone."

Leo thought about his father, his almost legendary defection and his own years of struggle to become recognized as a doctor in the US, and Leo saw the through line from his father's experience to Leo's own decision to become a doctor, how tightly his father's decisions were tied to his.

Nati continued, "I just couldn't imagine anyone throwing away a chance like that, because I would have never thrown away a chance like that. I thought that by pushing you toward a dream, I was doing something for your own good, even if it wasn't what you thought you wanted. I didn't want to be responsible for your regrets." She sighed. "But maybe, I was just projecting my priorities, and I'm sorry for that."

Leo took a deep breath to speak, but Nati put up a hand to stop him.

"But you owe me those days as well. I didn't tell you to run off and get married," she said, sniffling in the most undignified way, which melted him completely. He pulled her to him, letting her bury her face in his shoulder, use his shirt to dry her tears. "You gave up so easily."

"You told me you didn't love me." Nati opened her mouth to answer, but he stopped her. "No, it's my turn now. You were really convincing. But I should have trusted your actions. I was so defeated, I didn't look at what was in front of me, all the years you'd spent proving that you loved me. I shouldn't have been so quick to believe the worst-case scenario."

"I remember my resolve. I wouldn't have changed my mind." Nati snuffled, wiping her nose with her sleeve.

"No, maybe not," he answered, smoothing down her curls. "But I would have understood why you'd done it, instead of thinking that you'd simply stopped loving me. I kept asking myself what I'd done to make your feelings change and came up with answers that made no sense."

Nati set the box down on the nearest table and wrapped herself around Leo. "Being without you was the worst idea I've ever had. I promise I won't ever propose anything like that again."

Leo smiled into her hair, sinking into the way she smelled, the way she fit so perfectly in his arms. "And I promise I won't believe it if you do."

He tilted her head back, lowered his head and and kissed her, gentle and pure, like the love he felt for her. When pulled away, he said, "So give me the truth now. Do you still love me?"

Nati took his face in both her hands and gave him

a kiss that sent a frisson of pleasure to the very tips of his fingers and toes.

"I never stopped."

He hugged her, burying his face in her hair. "Neither did I."

They stood for a long while that way, as if separating might disrupt the fragile thing they'd managed to bring back to life. After a time, Leo lifted his head from her shoulder.

"You know, I kept all your gifts as well. They're in my bedroom."

Nati's eyes glittered with her brand of dangerous humor. "Hmm. Sounds like a strategy to get me into bed."

Leo raised a hand. "Guilty. It is totally a strategy to get you into bed. And to keep you there and never let you leave."

Nati quirked up the corner of her lips. "As long as you feed us. I never did learn how to cook."

Leo pulled her back into a fierce hug, squeezing her until she was gasping for air. "That's a favor I would be doing for us both."

Epilogue

Nati (six months later)

Paging Dr. Espinoza. Dr. Espinoza, please report to reception.

Nati leaned against the doorjamb of the reception area, trying to give Elena the most withering look possible. "This clinic is small enough that if just raise your voice just a little, Dr. Espinoza will hear you in the examination room."

Elena released the button of the intercom and turned a beaming smile in Nati's direction. "I know that, but it's the new intercom system, and it's so much fun to use!"

The news had come a few months after Leo had decided not to go back to California that East Ward's

Metropolitan Health Alliance had won the grant they'd so painstakingly applied for. It had been a true group project between the founders, Leo and his father. Even Leo's mother had grudgingly asked to look at the application to give feedback as well.

The money they were awarded allowed them to upgrade, among other things, their communications and record-keeping system, purchase the ultrasound machine, sign a contract for vaccine and lab supplies for the next year and give Elena the raise that she deserved. It turned out Leo was good at grant writing, a skill he had been putting to good use ever since to try and secure every penny they could to expand their operation until they were lucrative enough to form a trust that would allow the clinic to be funded indefinitely.

Leo found a position instead with New York Presbyterian. He was a surgeon on staff and had a ways to go before achieving the same position he'd had at UCLA, but because of that experience, he was on track to a position of greater responsibilities at the hospital.

"Elena?" Dr. Espinoza came around the corner, resting his hands on Nati's hips.

"Your next patient is waiting," Elena said, batting her eyes prettily. She'd taken a proprietary approach to Leo and Nati's relationship and wore perpetual heart-eyes every time they happened to be in the clinic together.

"And you needed to put me on blast for that?" he said, his voice full of humor for their favorite receptionist.

"I just want you to feel like you are at the hospital.

You know like when they page you because you're such an important surgeon and everybody is waiting for you in the operating room?"

"Not here." Nati laughed behind her hand while Leo shook his head. "Here, he's only a poor volunteer, like the rest of us."

Elena sighed. "But it sounds so official."

Leo chuckled at her antics. "Elena, only for emergencies, okay?"

"Yes, Dr. Espinoza," she said in a voice that indicated that she was not quite convinced of the validity of his request.

"Come here," Leo said to Nati when Elena had turned to the task of tending to her waiting patients. They stepped into the small business office, Leo closing the door behind Nati.

"Caio texted to say he was finished and sent us the pictures." He pulled out his phone and showed Nati the final arrangement for the nursery—including the bassinet that was Nati and Leo's baby-shower gift to match the crib Rafi and Étienne had chosen for the room. The nursery was decorated with a beautiful color scheme of yellow, orange and blue and included an old-fashioned wooden rocking chair from Papi and a combination bureau and changing table gifted by Val and Philip. Nati covered her mouth, touched by the care Leo had taken in making sure their gift would fit into the style of the room following the design elements Rafi and Étienne had chosen in the registry.

"Have Rafi and Étienne seen it yet?" Nati said.

Leo shook his head. "Val has been doing an epic job

of making sure to keep them busy with baby-clothes shopping. They'll see it when they get home tonight, just in time for the surprise baby shower."

"Leo! They're going to love it. I didn't think it would turn out like that, but now that I see it..." Nati swung her arms around Leo's neck, practically jumping on him and squeezed him so hard that he wheezed for air before she loosened her grip on him.

"Sorry," she giggled, joy and satisfaction making her giddy. "I'm just so excited for them."

"As you should be. This is a monumental moment in their life. I can't wait to see their faces."

"I know. You're so good like that." And he was. He was good at so many things. At being a good son, a good brother, a good friend. And the perfect lover for Nati, making her feel loved and cherished in a way she would never have confessed to needing. She could be competent and badass and ambitious but she also craved Leo's tenderness.

"So," Leo said, holding his arms loosely around Nati's waist. "When is it our turn?"

"Our turn?" Nati repeated, though she had an inkling of what he might be alluding to. Still, it was fun to hear him say it, and also a bit terrifying. Leo would always push Nati out of her comfort zone.

"Our turn. Your sister had her wedding. Rafi had a wedding and now a baby. When do we get ours?"

"Well, technically, I had a graduation party, and it was massive," Nati teased.

Leo bopped her on the nose. "That was only for

you. Remember, we are a team. Decisions only count if they include both of us."

Nati knew that lesson very well. No more thinking she knew better than him. No more galaxy brain, making decisions for others that they had a right to make on their own. They were in this adventure together, and she wasn't going to do anything to put that at risk, no matter what the consequences were. That's what being a team really meant.

Nati wiggled close, words far more innocent than what she was doing with her hips. "Then tell me. What's our party going to be for?"

Leo grinned as he took out a small black box. Nati rolled her eyes. He was so damn corny; of course, he'd propose to her in the office of the clinic they were expanding, the place of their shared dreams and the launching point for more dreams to come.

"Let me guess? It's the keys to my new motorcycle?" Nati laughed.

"New motorcycle? I'd like to see your old one, if you think you have all that courage to ride one," Leo retorted.

"A girl can dream, can't she?"

"Ducati. Next time." He pulled the box open and reached inside for the single solitaire ring. "See, this might rev something up after all, just not a bike."

"I'm going to engrave those words on my ring. Thank you for the memory." Nati stretched out her hand so he could slide the ring on to her ring finger.

"I'm taking that as a yes?" Leo asked.

Nati grabbed his face in both her hands and kissed

him as if her life depended on getting the kiss just right—which she did, because he moaned into her mouth like a benediction. When Nati released Leo's face, she sighed, leaving an errant kiss on his nose. "It's a yes."

He pulled her into his arms, all levity falling away. "I can't wait to spend the rest of my life with you, *mi colibri*."

"Our next great project," Nati said, smiling wet tears into the crook of his neck.

* * * * *

*She turned her back on love,
but her heart never forgot him.*

Read on for a sneak preview of
Starting Over at Trevino Ranch
by Amy Woods.

Chapter One

"Dad would for sure disown me if he saw what I'm doing right now," Gina Heron muttered under her breath as she scrolled down the page on her laptop screen. She must have started and abandoned the application for unemployment benefits at least ten times since breakfast, and she still couldn't seem to manage looking at it for more than a few minutes at a time without that familiar queasiness kicking up again.

"Well," Gina's sister, Sophie, responded from her spot facing a nearby bookshelf, where she'd been organizing new travel titles for the last half hour. "Dad's not here, is he? So, I wouldn't worry too much about him judging you." Her tone was gentle.

"I know, I know," Gina said, rubbing her temples as she released a sigh. "But he always chided us to 'never

take a handout' and in my head I've got a track on repeat of him saying, 'when things get hard, you've got
to pull yourself up by your bootstraps.'" She crossed
her arms for emphasis, just like Dad would have done.

Sophie put down the book she'd been holding and
moved behind Gina, wrapping her arms around her
sister's shoulders. "To that I would say, it's pretty damn
hard to pull them up when you don't have any straps
to speak of…not to mention boots."

Gina giggled softly, thankful for her older sibling's
steadfast sense of humor.

"Besides," Sophie continued, squeezing Gina's shoulders before heading back to her work, "it's not a handout. It's *your* tax money, there for a rainy day when
you need it." She picked up the next book from a box
near her feet, briefly studying the cover. "And goodness
knows you've had plenty of storms recently." Sophie
paused. "I just wish I could afford to hire you myself. It
would be so nice to have you working here with me—"
she turned and gave Gina an apologetic look "—for actual pay, I mean."

Gina closed the laptop with a little more force than
was probably necessary, earning a sideways glance
from a customer browsing the shelf closest to her.

That was enough for one day. The application
wasn't going anywhere, so she could continue staring at it tomorrow, hoping for some magic to happen
so she wouldn't actually have to go through with com-
pleting it. Her sister was right, of course, and in her
heart Gina knew she had no reason to feel ashamed
for needing a little help until she got back on her feet,

but a piece of her didn't want to admit defeat. Until she actually hit Submit, Gina could keep pretending that her life hadn't suddenly erupted into a total mess.

Standing up to stretch, she glanced out the front window of Sophie's small-town Texas bookshop, Peach Leaf Pages. Late afternoon sun washed over the sidewalk, and passersby, clad in T-shirts and shorts for the warm spring day, carried to-go cups of tea and coffee and brown paper bags of goodies from the café next door as they browsed the decorated storefronts along Main Street. A vanilla latte sounded perfect, but Gina cleared all thoughts of delicious hypothetical treats from her mind as she headed to Sophie's closet-sized office in the back to use her sister's one-cup coffee maker instead, visions of dwindling bank account balances dancing in her head.

Today marked one month since Gina's latest teaching contract had ended, and she had yet to land another offer.

Since graduating with her master's over a decade ago, she had moved seamlessly from one teaching position to the next. Specializing in English as a Second Language instruction for professional adults, her skill set had always been in demand overseas, and she had never struggled to find work. She'd spent many happy years bouncing across Asia, enjoying the incredible people, food and cultures she encountered each time she took a new contract, all the while promising herself she'd find a more permanent position and settle down one day in the distant future.

She had never imagined that the timing wouldn't be

her choice, that she'd be forced to stop moving against her will, before she was ready. But it seemed as though all of her colleagues with the placement agency had already found new positions or had chosen favorite locations to build lives. Meanwhile, Gina was stuck in her small hometown, treading water while her savings, and the little extra money she brought in from her tiny, word-of-mouth upholstery repair business, continued to decrease at an alarming rate.

Gina shook her head to clear away regret over a reality that no longer existed. She could keep her head in the clouds all day, but where would that get her? There was only one way to look at it now: at thirty-six, she would have to start all over again, and, having already achieved and lost her dream job, she had no idea how to do such a thing, or where to even begin. As thankful as she was that Sophie had been eager and happy to share her tiny space with her younger sister, Gina yearned desperately to regain her self-sufficiency.

"Oh, my gosh! I'm so sorry to hear that."

Gina turned abruptly at the worry in her sister's voice. A woman in her midsixties with cropped salt-and-pepper hair, sporting a stiff-looking back brace, grimaced in obvious pain as she spoke with Sophie, urgent tension in her voice.

"It's okay," the woman said, glancing woefully toward the children's section. "I'll heal in time, but I don't think I can sit through the reading today. I hate to leave you in the lurch like this, but I've got to get home and lie down. I'm due for meds soon and, until things get better, I'm having to take them like clockwork."

"Of course, Noreen," Sophie said, her words soothing as she followed the woman to the front of the store. "You should have just called, you poor thing. I would never have asked you to come in if I'd known you were in this condition. Dan must be worried sick."

Noreen waved a hand in dismissal. "Oh, he knows I'm a tough old bird. My back gives out every once in a while, so we know the ropes by now. The trouble is, I never know what's going to set the darn thing off. It'll be good as new before you know it, and I'll be back reading to the little ones."

"They'll miss you big time," Sophie said, holding the door open for the injured woman, who walked stiffly through, waving toward a sedan parked on the street just outside. The man in the vehicle—presumably her husband—got out of the driver's side and moved quickly to help his wife.

"There's Dan now," Noreen said. "Take care. My apologies again," she added with warm sincerity, hands clasped in front of her midsection. "I hope you can find somebody to take over."

"Oh, don't worry about us," Sophie called, smiling as Dan rushed over to take Noreen's hand. "You just concentrate on getting well."

As the couple got settled in their car and drove off, Sophie waved goodbye and closed the front door, setting off a pleasant chime of bells. She leaned against the solid oak and closed her eyes, pulling in a deep breath as if to center herself.

"They seem sweet," Gina mused, watching the car go.

"Yeah," Sophie agreed, opening her eyes as she

stood upright again. "They've been inseparable since they were kids."

A little shard of pain sliced through Gina. She had known a love like that once, long ago. Or at least she'd thought she had.

It became clear that Sophie's attempt to relieve her tension hadn't worked. She glanced in the distance over Gina's shoulder and bit her lip, worry filling her light brown eyes. Gina followed her gaze to the children's corner, a sweet alcove tucked in the space between two tall, blue-painted shelves full of picture and chapter books, adorned with cozy pillows, colorful carpet squares and sparkling strings of fairy lights.

"What's the matter?" Gina asked.

"Noreen was our children's reading hour volunteer." Sophie swallowed hard and looked down at her watch.

"So, you'll find another volunteer," Gina suggested. "Surely you've got a backup." But, as they'd been talking, Gina noticed that a few kids had started gathering on the carpets, their parents taking seats in a row of chairs set up just behind.

Sophie's head was moving slowly back and forth, and her teeth were making such a dent in her bottom lip that Gina worried she'd soon draw blood.

"So, I'm guessing…you don't have anyone else who can do it?"

"That's right," Sophie said, planting a hand against her forehead. "It's one of the million things on my to-do list that I keep thinking someday I'll have time for. Until you came to help out, it was about as long as Main Street, and it's getting shorter, but…"

"But you had a regular volunteer so that item wasn't at the top," Gina said, filling in with a growing sense of apprehension. She had an idea where this was going.

Sophie dove right in. "Come on, Gina, please?" She pulled up prayer hands in front of her pleading face.

"Um," Gina said, closing her own eyes so she wouldn't fall victim to her sister's huge, pleading, abandoned baby bunny ones, "I don't think I'm the right person for the job. You know I don't have much experience around kids." She swallowed anxiously.

"Please," Sophie said, the strain in her voice tugging hard at Gina's heartstrings. "You're a teacher, though. That's close enough, right?"

Gina stopped and dug in her heels, facing her sister as she steeled herself to be as firm as possible. "I teach business ESL *to adults*. Not exactly the same thing." She pulled her shoulders back, eyes darting about the shop as she desperately avoided meeting her sister's. "Now, if you'll excuse me, I believe I've got another round of job applications to fill out."

Sophie's expression softened. "Look. I know this is a little out of your wheelhouse. I wouldn't ask, but the kids are already here, and they'll be so disappointed if I cancel story hour."

Gina scanned the group of small humans as she considered her sister's request.

"Gina?" Sophie said quietly, reaching out to grasp her sister's arm.

"What?"

"It's just…you look nervous," Sophie said, a hint of a

giggle in her voice. "They're just children," she soothed. "They won't bite."

"You cannot guarantee that," Gina argued.

Sophie grimaced. "Well, you're right about that. But I can say they've never bitten Noreen, and that's something, right?"

Yeah, she looks sweet and all, but my sister can be pretty conniving, Gina thought.

Sophie assumed a serious expression and continued, "We're running out of time here, so are you going to help me or not? And, before you answer, remember whose couch you slept on last night."

Gina's mouth opened wide and her eyes narrowed. "Oh, that's low, Soph," she chided, clicking her tongue, even as she silently prepared to give in to the inevitable. She knew she couldn't leave her sister like this, not when there was a crowd gathered already and parents were starting to check the time impatiently.

Gina knew Sophie had put her heart, soul and years of saved-up dollars into her bookstore, and she'd worked her butt off to get it off the ground, even as nearly everyone around her said that brick-and-mortar book sales were a thing of the past. As she watched Sophie wring her hands, Gina knew what she had to do, and dammit she would do it.

"Fine," she said, her insides melting as Sophie's face lit up with gratitude, her pale cheeks regaining the color they'd lost. "But you owe me."

Sophie started to speak, probably to remind Gina again about the couch and the free roof over her head, but Gina stopped her.

"You owe me." She rolled her shoulders a few times and cracked her knuckles, preparing for the lions' den. "Two margaritas as soon as we close up. No negotiations. Take the deal or I'll walk." Gina fixed a steely gaze on her sister.

Sophie's lips trembled as though she might laugh. The nerve.

"I mean… I won't walk far, but, you know…back to the office to work on the books or something," Gina said, afraid she'd been a tad too harsh.

Only a tad, though.

"Deal," Sophie said, holding out her hand.

Gina shook it, very reluctantly, glaring additional death rays at her only sibling.

"Wonderful. Thank you so much!" Sophie bounced up and down. "By the way, the book is on the big chair in front of the kids." She snorted. "You'll be reading, *Tomorrow I'll be Brave*, by Jessica Hische."

A favorite of her sister's, Gina knew the book well, and the pertinence of its title, as well as the book's message that it's okay to be scared when trying new things, did not escape her. With a deep breath, she crossed her fingers and hoped she could live up to it.

No matter how hard he tried, Alex Trevino seemed doomed to fail when it came to getting his niece and nephew to their various activities on time.

He'd always taken pride in being early to events and appointments. As his *abuelo* taught him growing up: "on time equals late, and early equals on time"—advice he took seriously and continued to live by, and that had served him well for all of his thirty-seven years. Advice that seemed impossible to live up to when it came to kids.

His heart softened as he glanced in the rearview mirror at ten-year-old Eddie and six-year-old Carmen, wondering how it could possibly have taken so long to get them into his pickup. There must be some sort of time vortex when it came to children; it took twice as long to get them to accomplish anything as you thought it would, and even if you started getting ready early, the extra time somehow didn't add up the way it should, as if each minute flew by in only thirty seconds.

He must have made himself chuckle because Eddie asked, "What's so funny, Uncle Alex?"

Seeing no other vehicles on the sleepy ranch road, Alex turned quickly to smile at his nephew. The little boy had inherited the Trevino family's dark hair and eyes, and his mother's endearing dimples. "Oh, nothing much, bud." Alex turned back to face the road. "Are you guys excited about story hour?" he asked hopefully. He would do anything in his power to cheer them up these days.

"Meh," Eddie responded. "Story hour is for little kids, but I'll go because Carmen needs me to look out for her."

At this declaration, a lump formed in Alex's throat. It was a tender sentiment from a protective big brother, even if it was only half true. He knew for a fact that Eddie, an avid reader since age five, absolutely loved story hour, and really, any story he could hear, see, or get his hands on. That kid was going to become some kind of writer when he grew up. Alex would bet his family's ranch on it. On top of that, Eddie was just an all-around good kid, who had put his whole heart into looking after his little sister since their parents—Alex's older brother and sister-in-law—had lost their lives in a plane crash the year before.

Becoming Eddie and Carmen's guardian had been a whirlwind of lawyers, documents and packing up their things to move in with him, the tasks providing an escape from his own grief. Having gone from bachelor to caregiver overnight, Alex hadn't had a chance to deal with his own pain, and, while he'd been thankful for the distraction at the time, some days he wondered if he should spend some time finally processing everything that had happened, maybe even get some counseling…if he could ever find a spare moment.

Alex turned onto Main Street and located a parking spot near Peach Leaf Pages, then got out to help the kids from the back seat, taking a small hand in each of his. As the bell on the shop door chimed, announcing their arrival, Alex quickly noted that the children's area was already full, and the other kids were fully engrossed in the story.

So much for sneaking in without disruption.

He knew he shouldn't be surprised. Noreen Connelly, retired sixth-grade teacher—his, actually—was a stickler for punctuality, even when she wasn't on the clock, which meant this marked their third week of making a far more conspicuous entrance than he would have liked.

Oh well, Alex thought, guiding Eddie and Carmen toward the reading circle, hoping there was still a spot left for each of them. Not much could be done about it now. As much as he'd like to, he couldn't turn back time any more than Cher could.

"Okay, guys," he said softly. "Let's be as quiet as possible so we don't interrupt the story."

He gently squeezed each child's hand and led the way.

"But how will we know what's going on?" Eddie asked quietly, mild frustration in his voice. "The new lady's already started reading."

"Yeah!" agreed Carmen, much, *much* less quietly than her brother, prompting an aggravated "Shhh!" from someone in the group.

Probably Kenneth, resident taskmaster. Aged five. Relentless enforcer of story hour etiquette, with a disapproving scowl that burned all the way to your toes.

Alex briefly closed his eyes, drawing in a breath. Okay, so maybe they needed to spend a little more time working on inside voices, at least before his niece started kindergarten the following year. He was definitely in support of a woman with a strong voice who knew how to use it…just…maybe not during story time.

"Carmen, sweetheart, let's try to whisper," Alex said, demonstrating. "And, Eddie, it's okay. We're only a few minutes behind. I'm sure you'll be able to catch up on the plot in no time."

He got his two settled with the other kids and moved farther back to find a seat among the other parents and guardians, who, thankfully, adjusted knees and purses to let him pass, probably having been in his shoes before. Maybe not as often as he had, but still.

Smiling gratefully, Alex finally slid into a chair of his own, just as something Eddie had said before caught his attention.

What *new lady*?

Noreen had been the only story hour volunteer every time Alex had brought Eddie and Carmen for the past several months, and as far as he knew, she had no desire to give up her position. The kids adored Mrs. Connelly. She did all the voices in the books, was so animated that Alex was certain she could have had an Oscar-worthy acting career if the teaching hadn't worked out, and she even used props and wore homemade, highly accurate character costumes. Likely there weren't many people lining up to take Noreen's place in the high energy, paycheckless endeavor. Plus kids that age were a tough crowd. Alex was pretty sure they could smell fear, and probably parental inadequacy too, which he had plenty of.

Taking *guardianship* of Eddie and Carmen had been an easy choice; he loved his niece and nephew and it was simply the right thing to do. He'd been in their lives from infancy, spending time with them at family events, never missing a single birthday or milestone, and babysitting when his brother and sister-in-law went on anniversary trips. Taking *care* of Eddie and Carmen, on the other hand…nothing had ever been more challenging.

Having wanted his own kids someday, Alex had

never been naive enough to think that parenting would be an easy job, but he hadn't even remotely grasped how utterly *big* it was. Not just the day-to-day tasks involved in keeping two small humans alive, dressed and fed, and getting them to the places they needed to go, but the deeper stuff. The questions he couldn't answer. The philosophies he hadn't yet considered about how best to develop these two into good people, good citizens, good stewards of their gifts and resources who cared for their community and planet and…it was a *lot*.

He wasn't prepared, and he was slowly beginning to understand that maybe nobody was. Maybe nobody *could* be, not fully anyway.

In the meantime, he did the only thing he knew, which was to give his best moment by moment and hope it added up to something that would serve those kids well, because they'd sure as hell been through enough already.

A cheerful voice pulled his attention back to the present. Wait…there was something familiar about that voice. It set off a mosaic of memories—little pieces that didn't quite add up to anything solid, but made him feel a thousand hazy things at once. Spring rainstorms and a majestic show of lightning from the vantage of a barn loft; a summer day on a dock down at the reservoir, a beach towel for a picnic blanket; the high school football stadium, just before kickoff, a small hand in his and a soft voice encouraging him, easing the jitters that sometimes got so bad his stomach would hurt just before he had to go out on the field…

That voice. He'd recognize it anywhere.

And yet.

Alex looked up in disbelief. It couldn't be her. She was gone—had been gone for years now. Not enough to make him forget, unfortunately, but enough to ease the hurt to a point that he'd been able to build a life that didn't include her.

It was then he noticed that the reading had stopped—in fact, all noise around him had ceased—and the entire row of parents, the kids on the carpet and the customers milling around the bookshelves…all had their eyes on him. Briefly, it crossed his mind that this level of unwanted attention should make him pretty damn uncomfortable, except that he couldn't really process any of it.

Not when Gina Heron, the love of his life, the same girl he hadn't seen in nearly two decades and had in fact never expected to see again, was staring straight at him.

"Um, excuse me, miss," interjected Kenneth the future hall monitor, pointer finger raised. "The story?"

Unable to take his eyes off her, Alex watched as Gina cleared her throat and forced her concentration back onto the slim chapter book that sat closed in front of her. Sliding from her lap as she startled, it took a dive and landed with a quiet *smack* at her feet, splitting the continued silence. She glanced down, not seeming to register what had happened until a little girl picked up the book, handed it back, patted her knee reassuringly and returned to a spot on the carpet.

Gina shook her head. "Thank you," she said to the little girl, eyes wide.

"Uh, okay," Gina said, thumbing through the pages until she found where she'd left off. "Let's continue."

Meeting Alex's gaze one more time before quickly pulling her eyes away, she picked up where she'd left off, her voice shaking a little from time to time until she regained her footing.

Alex closed his eyes and pinched his thigh, hard, through his worn jeans, but when he opened them back up, she was still there. Daring to look to his left and right, he was relieved to discover that he no longer captured the attention of everyone in the room. The parents around him had resumed reading email on their cell phones and the shoppers were once again browsing, no longer curious about the sudden silence in the children's corner, and all was as it should be.

Except that Gina Heron, the woman he'd promised his heart to at age eight, the woman who'd turned down his marriage proposal after they'd planned a life together—the woman he'd tried with all his might and yet failed to stop loving—was apparently back in town. Add to this that not a single soul, not even Gina's sister, Sophie, who knew damn well that he and the kids showed up weekly for story hour, had thought to pass along this epic news.

To make matters worse, seeing her didn't just bring back all the bad stuff, all the heartache she'd caused. Looking at her now—that halo of untamable, curly gold hair, the almond-shaped light brown eyes that nothing slipped past, and those sweet soft curves he'd lost himself in so many times—it was easy to pretend that not a moment had been lost between them.

Too easy.

The room began to spin a little, and Alex's breath came in shallow spurts.

He couldn't just leave. It wouldn't be fair to the kids, who needed routine and consistency and who looked forward to story hour. It would be selfish to disrupt their time just because he couldn't manage to get it together. All because of a woman he should have gotten over ages ago.

Chapter Two

I am going to kill you, Sophie Alice Heron, and scatter your remains in Marty Montalvo's chicken yard, Gina thought, seething, even as she wondered whether or not the lovably eccentric older guy still named his favorite fowl after country western singers. Her personal favorites had been Waylon Hennings, Dwight Yolkum and Tanya Clucker.

Focusing on the task at hand, she plastered on a smile for the kids. They didn't need to know that the person reading them a cute story harbored homicidal thoughts toward her older sister.

Her traitorous older sister.

How could Sophie not have told her that Alex might bring his kids to reading hour? How could Sophie not have told her that *Alex had kids*? He had to, because he was sitting back there in the parent chairs, staring down at the floor to avoid making eye contact with her.

For the love of all things holy, her sister owed her that much.

Alex had been the love of her life, and he had broken her heart. Even though she'd had to do it, leaving town, leaving him, after graduation had torn her to pieces, so many in fact that she'd almost failed at putting them back together. This information wasn't something her sister could have just forgotten, and as soon as these kids stopped staring at her, and the chapter was over…oh, she and Sophie would have words.

Just don't look at him and it will be easier, Gina told herself. She only had to get through this, and she could walk straight past the front desk and right up the narrow staircase at the back that led to her sister's apartment above the shop. It wasn't that hard.

Thanking the stars when she saw that the next page was only half-filled with words, the bottom portion a blank void of white space, Gina managed to finish the last bit of the story without having a panic attack or making a run for the door.

"And that's it for this week," she said, her voice so loud and unnaturally pleasant she was pretty sure she scared a few of the kids. "I'm sure…*someone* will be here next week to pick up where we've left off."

As the little ones began to disperse and reunite with their parents, her eyes darted around the bookstore to locate her sister, but her vision was cut off when a girl Gina guessed to be about six years old came up and stood before her, shifting from leg to leg.

Crap, Gina thought. She'd done her sisterly duty and filled in for the absentee story hour reader. Surely she didn't have to entertain follow-up questions. Kids always seemed to cut right to the chase, to ask the hardest questions—ones she, even as an adult, never quite knew how to answer.

"Miss?" the girl said, bouncing on her heels.

Gina closed her eyes to calm her racing heart, then opened them slowly.

"Yes?" she asked, meeting the little girl's eyes. They were umber in color and warm, set deep in a heart-shaped, tawny-beige face. As much as she didn't want to be, Gina surprised herself by responding to the kid's widening grin with one of her own. The girl gingerly placed a little hand on Gina's knee.

"I really liked how you read the story," she said, before turning on her heel and running straight for Alex.

Of course.

Gina's smile dissolved.

It was ridiculous not to have recognized those familiar features, even in another person's face. The hairs on the back of her neck stood as realization settled in. *Of course* Alex would have moved on, met someone else and started a life without her—a life that obviously included children.

What had she expected? That he would, what...wait for her? Really. She'd never given him any indication that she would come back and, in fact, hardheaded and stubborn at eighteen, she'd promised quite the opposite. It was a move that brought her sorrow nearly every day since. She'd made the decision to walk away from a lifetime with Alex; at the time it had seemed the right choice, at least to her young heart.

Growing up in Peach Leaf, with a distant, reluctant father had been difficult and isolating. Small towns weren't always friendships and potlucks and festivals. Sometimes it was loneliness, being surrounded by people who knew what was going on at home, who saw their dirty clothes and unkempt hair and knew how hard things were for her and Sophie, but who hadn't lifted a finger to help because it might have gotten messy.

Staying and building a life among the prying, judgmental eyes of her neighbors had never appealed to Gina, especially not when there was a great big world out there she wanted to explore. A life of travel and new experiences had called to her, and she hadn't been able—hadn't wanted—to resist.

Yes, there were moments here and there when she questioned her decision, but that's what life was: a series of choices. When you made one, there wasn't always the opportunity to turn back, and the years were too short to waste wondering what might have been. So, you moved on, and you did the best you could.

And yet here she was in the same room with him again, a place she never thought she'd be, and he was walking in her direction.

"Hey, Gina," Alex said softly, his expression guarded.

The simplest greeting, and yet it had the power to unravel her. The years of wondering whether she'd made the right move, of thinking about him every day whether she wanted to or not, of not being strong enough to throw out that old football jersey that followed her from one apartment to another no matter how far back she shoved it in a drawer...

Looking straight into his eyes, unable to find the right words to say, her heart would know him anywhere. It was Alex. The Alex she'd loved so long ago.

Time had done little to change his features. He had the same deep brown eyes and tawny skin as the tiny girl who clung to his leg—though the sun had burnished his a shade darker—and the muscles under his shirt and faded jeans were hardened from ranch work.

He must have done what he'd promised, she thought, and taken over his family's decades-old business. It had been a point of contention between them all those years before, but she could see now that it appeared to suit him.

"Hi," she responded, her voice surprisingly steady considering the surge of complicated and confusing emotions swirling around in her brain.

Gina wished she'd never come back to this town, with its inescapable memories and history that had a grip on her. She knew she didn't want to spend her whole life in Peach Leaf. That's why she'd left all those years ago—to escape. At the same time, it was home, and everybody knew you could only run so far from it. And the biggest part of her history was standing right in front of her, pulling her back into a world she'd been so sure she wanted out of. So sure…

"So, you're the new storyteller?" Alex asked, studying her with an intensity she'd always found unsettling. He had known her so well for so long that the smallest change in her expression could tell him what she was thinking without a word spoken. It was both overwhelmingly comforting to be known that deeply, and disquieting because he was the one person she could never truly hide from.

"Ah, no. Definitely not," Gina answered. "I don't have much experience with kids."

"Odd way to spend an afternoon then, don't you think?" Alex mused. His expression had softened and a corner of his lips ticked upward.

He was teasing her, she understood suddenly, inviting her to lighten the moment with him, and she was thankful for the gesture.

"Let's just say it wasn't exactly in my calendar," she said, grinning, her nerves loosening a little as she talked. "Sophie needed me to fill in for Mrs...."

"Connelly," Alex finished for her.

"Right," Gina said. "Noreen injured her back, so here I am."

"Sophie owes you one, doesn't she?" he asked, his lips splitting into a grin that reminded her why she'd been drawn to him in the first place.

Oh jeez. If she had any sense, she would walk straight out that door. Anything but stand there and watch those dimples start to get under her skin again. If she had any sense...

"You bet she does," Gina answered. And it was the last thing she could think of to say because, really, where would this end? What was the point of having a conversation at all, when she had no intention of digging up the past?

He was watching her again, little grooves at the corners of his intelligent brown eyes telling her he had at least some idea of her unspoken thoughts.

"Well," she said, "I've got to put this book away and get back to work."

His eyebrows perked up. "Oh, you're working for Sophie now?" Alex asked. "I know she's needed help for a while. This place gets so busy on the weekends. It's nice that you came back to town to do that for her," he said warmly, a hint of deeper interest underneath the polite, safe statement.

In lieu of explaining, Gina simply offered a resigned smile and pointed to the shelf behind him. "It's nice to see you again, Alex. If you'll excuse me, I've got to shelve this and—"

"Get back to work." He nodded. "I know."

He moved closer to her, so close that she could smell the cinnamon mints he'd always favored. The scent, once a balm to her nerves, now prompted a wave of sadness that hit her like a storm wall.

Tight-lipped, she waved the book in front of him and ducked her head to silently pass by.

"Here," he said, his voice soothing as he followed. "Let me help."

"I don't—"

"Please." Gina heard so much more than a simple word when he said it.

Avoiding his gaze, she held out the volume and Alex gripped it, his fingers grazing hers, their touch no less charged now than it had always been.

Pulling it gently out of her hand, Alex walked toward the bookshelves in the children's area, Gina unable to keep from following closely in his wake like a tugboat tailing a ship. He scanned the titles until he found the spot where it belonged, then used his thumb to mark the space.

"Ah," he said. "Here we go."

Reaching up, he almost had the book in place when suddenly, the little boy he'd brought with him appeared at his side and gave a tug on Alex's jeans. Startled, Alex dropped the book, which bounced right off Gina's head before landing on the carpet with a thud.

"Ow!" she cried out.

Gina had only just reached up to rub the newly sore spot when Alex's fingers grazed her hair, his hands gently cupping her face.

"Oh my God, I'm so sorry. Are you okay?" He bent down to stare into her eyes and all she could do was stare back, neither of them realizing for several seconds that any time had passed at all. He was comforting her, caring for her as he would have if they'd never parted ways, and she let him, completely unable to move herself to stop it.

When Alex caught himself and pulled his hands away abruptly, tucking them into his pockets as if they burned, his reaction smarted far more than the bump on her head.

Gathering her wits as she brushed stray curls from her brow, Gina nodded. "Yeah, I'm all right. It's just a little sore."

"I'm so sorry, Gina. I never meant to—"

The sound of giggling erupted behind them, and they looked down to see Alex's kids doing a very poor job controlling their laughter.

Alex frowned and chided softly, "Hey, guys, it's not nice to laugh when someone gets hurt."

But it was too late. The musical sound of the kids' giggling mixed with Alex's very serious expression, plus the need to release some of the morning's tension and the awkwardness of running into her childhood sweetheart, let something loose inside Gina. In a single moment she was laughing as well, and the kids were laughing even harder, and then Alex was laughing, too, and…

"It's really okay," she said when she'd calmed down enough to speak. "I know you didn't mean to hurt me."

"I truly didn't," Alex said. His smile faded and he looked at her for a long time, making her very self-aware. "And I am sorry."

"We're sorry too," said the little boy who looked like a miniature version of Alex. "We didn't mean to laugh. I hope you're okay." He glanced shyly down at his sneakers.

Gina's throat went dry, and there was a tickle behind her eyes. "Oh…that's okay," she said. "I know it's hard not to laugh when someone gets bonked on the head, and I'm not hurt."

"Aren't you going to kiss it?" the little girl asked suddenly, twirling a finger in her dark hair as her eyes darted between the grown-ups.

"Uh…what?" Alex asked, blinking as the tops of his ears turned pink.

Gina folded her lips together and put a hand over them, trying hard not to smile.

"Kiss the nice lady's head," the girl said, pointing

toward Gina's noggin with an exasperated huff, as if she could hardly be bothered explaining the obvious. "When I get hurt, you kiss it and make it better. Aren't you going to kiss her head where you dropped the book? You have to make it better." She raised her palms as if to say, "Duh!"

Gina supposed she could have made things easier for Alex, but it was far more satisfying to watch him squirm. What happened next, though, she couldn't have prepared for.

"She's right, you know," Alex said, his eyes softening as he narrowed the distance between them, causing her breath to hitch. "I did in fact drop a book on you, and who knows, you might even have a knot there soon thanks to me, so the least I can do is…"

Reaching out to gently grasp the tops of her arms, he leaned over and pressed his lips to her crown, holding them there for longer than he should have, but perhaps not as long as she would have liked.

"All better now," Alex whispered, brushing his fingers against her cheek before pulling away slowly, his deep brown eyes meeting hers.

So much passed between them in that single look that Gina couldn't bring herself to speak, despite her mouth opening and closing several times. Alex, of course, noticed this and seemed to take joy in the fact that he still had the ability to undo her, a fact that would have annoyed her if she'd been able to feel anything other than pure shock.

The kids were staring wide-eyed when Gina finally

regained control of her body and glanced their way. "I, uh, I guess I'll, uh…"

"It was good to run into you, Gina," Alex said, his eyes darkened with mischief. "We'll see you around."

Alex reached out his hands and the kids took one each, waving at her as the little family headed back through the store. When they reached the front door, he glanced back once before opening it to leave, his expression too complicated to read.

"Not if I can help it," she whispered to herself as the door closed behind them.

Seeing him this once had shaken the already wobbly ground she'd been teetering on since losing her job. Until a month ago, there had always been a next step, a new job in a new country, another destination to run off to. Gina didn't know if she had the courage to face the past, to unpack her troubled childhood and the people she blamed for looking the other way, to make amends for leaving Sophie—and Alex—for so long without ever stopping in to see if they were okay.

A question nagged at her from somewhere deep inside.

How will I cope if I have to stay still for a while?

"I hear what you're saying," mused Vanessa Green, Alex's best friend and owner of Knot Your Average Crafts, a yarn and crochet shop on Main Street. "It's just that I don't believe you."

Vanessa raised her eyebrows pointedly as she continued sorting through a new shipment of patterns.

The shop was quiet on a Tuesday morning. Alex

had stopped by to say hello after taking the kids to their dentist appointments. He'd assigned the morning's tasks at the ranch to his most trusted hand, but he knew from experience that not being there to participate in the work himself would nag at him for the rest of the day. Then again, so would his best friend if she knew they'd come into town without stopping by.

Alex threw up his hands in defeat. One of the things he loved most about Van was her straightforward honesty, but that didn't mean it was always easy to swallow.

"I mean it," he said, pushing back, still reeling from seeing Gina only a few days before. "Every word. I definitely kissed her."

"On the head," added Carmen absently, utterly enchanted as she stroked the new purple-and-turquoise shawl Vanessa had made for her.

Alex had known the second his friend lovingly bestowed the colorful gift on her that his niece would be wearing it nonstop for at least a month, and he wouldn't be allowed to wash it even though he'd been given very clear instructions on *how to do it the right way*. His standard ranch clothes weren't exactly high maintenance, so when he became a father figure he'd made a mistake here and there in the laundry department, among others, and boy had he gotten an earful.

Vanessa's husband, Darian, had been the accountant for Trevino Ranch for nearly a decade and the first time Alex had invited the couple and their two kids over for dinner, Vanessa and Alex had bonded instantly over their shared love of mystery novels and true crime. The families had been inseparable ever since, and Alex knew he would be completely lost without the couple's patient advice and steadfast support when it came to parenting.

Though Alex's mother insisted on helping as much as possible, she was getting older and had already done the work of raising children of her own. He knew she adored spending time with her grandchildren, but Alex didn't want to take advantage of her generosity, and he felt that she deserved to enjoy her golden years as she pleased.

He loved Carmen and Eddie, deeply, and he was more than happy to be their guardian, but when he'd imagined having a family of his own, those dreams had always included a partner, someone to share the burden of managing his family's ranch, as well as the challenges that came with raising small children.

Vanessa stopped unpacking the new stock and looked straight at him, her mahogany eyes wide, tight curls bouncing as she tilted her head. "So, the kids really did see you kiss your long-lost high school sweetheart?" she asked, pointing a finger between them and him. "On the head, apparently?"

Gina was so much more than a high-school flame, but Alex just rolled his eyes. "Makes me feel so good that you'll take the word of a six-year-old over your best friend."

Van's lips rose in a mischievous grin. "I know I can always trust Carmen to tell it like it is."

"Truer words…" Alex said, sharing Van's smile. Carmen told the truth, loud and proud, no matter where they were, who the audience was, or how embarrassing it might be.

"I guess it was just an in-the-moment reaction," he explained, shrugging as he stuffed nervous hands into his pockets. "I know it doesn't make sense, but after all these years of not seeing her, it felt like…no time had passed." He couldn't help the tickle inside his chest at the thought of the woman he'd loved so much for so long. She'd hardly looked any different, which added to the strange feeling that maybe almost two decades hadn't actually slid by in which they'd built separate lives. If anything, the added years only agreed with her, as if the passage of time had simply polished her best features.

Something flickered across Vanessa's expression, and Alex knew she worried about him. And to be fair, why wouldn't she? While he tried not to dwell on the past too much, and didn't see the point in wishing for a life he'd once dreamed of, he had certainly talked about Gina a few times, and Van knew his heart had never fully healed after the breakup.

It probably seemed troublesome to Van that he had made such a bold move when keeping his distance would've been a smarter choice. If Gina was back in town, regardless of how long she planned to stay, he couldn't expect to avoid her entirely but he sure as hell could've been a little bit smarter, a little more protective of his banged-up heart. Because along with the joy of seeing her again—that frisson of happiness at the sight of a face he held dear—there was an ache as well, of old wounds resurfaced.

"Listen," Vanessa said, her voice warm with friendship but nonetheless firm, "I'm not going to tell you what's best for you—you're a grown man and that's your job to figure out—but I am going to tell you to be careful, because I do *want* what's best for you and I don't want to see you hurt again." She shoved the box aside and put her palms down on the counter in front of her. "I wasn't here when you guys were together, but I know that what happened between you left scars you've worked hard to heal. Don't forget the weight of that work."

Alex nodded with gratitude, swallowing hard. Her words were so insightful that he had to take a deep breath to regroup.

"Enough about my past," he said, changing the subject as he went to pull Carmen's perpetually sticky hands from a boxed set of crochet hooks and redirected her to join her brother. Eddie was sorting glass beads by color and texture, a task Van always left open for him when they came in, knowing how much he enjoyed the soothing activity. "I want to hear what's new at Chez Green, and if you've read anything good recently."

Van's eyes lit up, and Alex was grateful for her willingness to switch tracks with him.

"Nothing much at home. Darian's still trying to rope me into trying his raw food recipes and I'm still not having it, and yes, I have read something good! There's a new one out about a group of community college students who went missing from Peach Leaf in the seventies. Of course, I won't tell you how the case went down." She winked and wiped her hands on her slacks, disappearing into her office at the back for a second before rejoining him with a hardcover, which she handed over. "I didn't want to wait for the library to order it, so I went ahead and bought it for myself. You can borrow it when I'm done, which won't be long because it's nearly impossible to put down and I'm sneaking a few pages any chance I can."

He read the inside cover and handed it back. "Looks intriguing," he said. "I need something to distract me anyway…from things."

"This'll do it. Made me never want to go for a walk in the woods again, though, I have to say," Van added with a little shiver.

"Perfect," Alex answered, and the two friends shared a smile just before the shop door chimed announcing a customer, or, just as likely in Peach Leaf, a friend.

Alex and Van looked up at the same time.

A talented businesswoman and welcoming person in general, Van called out a friendly hello and, tossing a quick glance back at Alex, headed toward her new customer to see if she could offer any help. He, on the other hand, stood completely still, as if one of the kids had hot-glued his shoes to the floor.

Gina.

Don't miss Starting Over at Trevino Ranch
*by Amy Woods, wherever Harlequin® Special
Edition books and ebooks are sold.
www.Harlequin.com.*

HARLEQUIN
PLUS

Try the best multimedia subscription service for romance readers like you!

Read, Watch and Play.

Experience the easiest way to get the romance content you crave.

Start your **FREE TRIAL** at
<u>www.harlequinplus.com/freetrial</u>.